OUT

OF

TIME

LORETTA
LIVINGSTONE

Cover by Chris Graham of TSRA Book Covers
www.http://thestoryreadingapeblog.com/authors-resources-
central/tsra-doings/

ISBN: **1500666343**
ISBN-13: **978-1500666347**

For Liz, my best friend for more years than I can remember.

PROLOGUE

Early May 1191
Near Sparnstow Abbey

Giles was annoyed. He had been intending to spend some time at his manor, too often neglected of late, but John had summoned him, with a handful of others, to act as escort.

He had not been present at John's meeting but, to judge by his expression, things had not gone well. The whole thing was beginning to smell suspiciously of treason. *A murrain on John and his accursed intrigues.* Giles did not want to be involved in this but could see no way out.

He allowed himself to lag behind, a sour expression on his face. John noticed and slowed his mount until he, too, had dropped behind the others. Nudging close to Giles, he snarled, "Remove that look of disgust, de Soutenay, and remember to whom you swore allegiance."

Giles was about to point out that allegiance did not include treason, when his horse whinnied in protest as a bee buzzed around its ears. Giles swatted at it, and the bee moved irritably away. Attracted by a bright splash of colour, it flew to investigate.

John, resplendent in a mantle of saffron silk, made to brush the bee away as it landed on his tunic. The bee, already annoyed, reacted instinctively. John gave a yelp of pain, and his horse reared. Giles smirked and rode to join the others in the entourage, leaving John swearing as his head cracked on an overhanging bough.

John brought his mount under control and, rubbing his brow, cantered to the head of the troop. Half a mile down the road, Giles' amusement turned to alarm as John fell from his horse.

CHAPTER ONE

Early May 2006
Sparnstow Abbey

"Go on, then. Try to stay out of trouble."

"Mum!" Chloe glared at me, exasperation oozing from her. "You are just so embarrassing."

I ignored her huff. "And…"

"And *yes*! I *have* got Shannon's epinephrine jab. Do I ever forget? Seriously?" She stood there, hands on hips, bristling with fourteen-year-old outrage.

Shannon has a rather scary allergy to bee stings. The whole family are trained to know how to deal with it, and, haphazard as Chloe can be on occasion, she is very reliable where Shannon is concerned. We don't want to wrap the poor kid in cotton wool. Nevertheless, I like to be within range of them both.

Thinking of the spare I should be carrying, I rummaged in my bag – yes, there it was, along with the other paraphernalia we mums carry around with us. It always surprises me that you can't tell which women are mothers by the longer length of one arm from hauling all the family necessities around year after year.

"Off you go, then. I'll stay here and read. It's much too hot for me. Have fun."

They each blew me a kiss and scampered across the grass.

I sat in the car and dug out my novel. Peace at last. Opening the book, I lost myself in its pages…for about twenty minutes. Overhead, the sun seemed even brighter than it had been at noon. It beat down, unhindered by clouds.

Heaving a sigh, I fanned myself with the book. Even with all the doors thrown open and my legs sticking out as far as they could go, it was stifling.

Groaning, I got out. It made little difference. Why on earth were there no trees in this car park? I grabbed a diaphanous piece of cotton which I'd tossed into the car at the last moment thinking it might come in handy to sit on or maybe throw over my shoulders to protect them from burning. My legs were ok. Sweaty but shaded in a sage green, ankle-length dress, at least I wouldn't have to worry about sunscreen for them. Sweat trickled down between my shoulder blades. It was no good. I couldn't sit here waiting for the kids; I needed to go and find some shade.

We were visiting an old, ruined abbey. Both my girls were history crazy at the moment, thanks to a particularly inventive teacher. I hadn't been able to face tramping around the grounds with them, but twenty minutes of sitting in a tin-can in the full glare of an over-zealous sun had changed my mind.

Not a cloud softened the azure sky; not a breath of wind stirred the air. Even the birds seemed too hot to sing. Wearily, I threw the shawl-cum-scarf over my shoulders, then removed the satnav, stuffing it in my bag. Locking the car, I plodded across the wide expanse of grass to the ruins of the Abbey where, at least, I could sit in the shade of a nice, cool, stone wall.

It wasn't a very large abbey, well the ruins weren't, but apparently, it had been quite well loved in its day.

The attendant, in his small ticket office, looked even hotter than I felt.

"That'll be £10 love, please. Phew! Wish I had a fan in here," he gasped, flapping at himself with a brochure.

He held out a sweaty paw, and I dropped my cash into it with a sympathetic smile. As he pressed a button, I pushed at the turnstile, which made an agonised squeal as though even it was protesting about working today.

Once inside, I wandered around a bit but there were far too many people for my liking. I was about to pass the tea rooms when I paused. There were a few unoccupied chairs inside and none at all outside, except for those few with no shady umbrella. I dithered as I took in the long queue of noisy kids and grumpy parents snaking out of the door and a couple of angry wasps buffeting against the window, but I could see there was an ice-cream freezer chest inside. *It'll be worth it,* I promised myself.

As I reached the head of the queue and pointed out my choice, the lady behind the counter gave me a harassed smile. "You're lucky I've got any left, love; it's a madhouse here today. I'm tempted to lock the door, climb in the freezer and eat them all myself." She took my money and handed over an orange lolly. "You know what you want to do with that? Before you take off the paper, run it round your wrists. That'll cool you down nicely…" She broke off to glare at a child who was carelessly discarding a wrapper. "Oi! Pick that paper up and put it in the bin…and you! Get your sticky mitts out of my freezer. I'll get it out for you. Which one did you want? Honestly, kids!" She turned her attention back to the queue behind me, dismissing me with a wave of her hand.

Taking her advice, I discovered she was right – it did cool me down a bit, running it round my wrists. I peeled off the paper, chucked it in the bin and bit into the ice-cold oranginess. *Lovely.*

Next, I wanted to locate my girls. Chloe, who has decided to call herself Eleanor thanks to an inspired idea of the aforementioned history teacher who let them choose their favourite medieval name to be used during her class and, it seems, at home, was likely to be the ringleader in any escapades they were up to. Chloe is a natural leader. Shannon, a couple of years younger, is content to trail in her wake. Shannon, by the way, is now Rohese – there not being many Shannons around in medieval times according to her sister. I wouldn't know. Not being much of a history buff, they could tell me anything and I'd believe it.

Of course, Chloe would choose Eleanor; it is the name of some medieval queen, she tells me. Apparently, she was one of the most beautiful women in history. Also talented. Not particularly given to modesty, our Chloe/Eleanor. She tells me my name doesn't need a medieval overhaul. My mother, Ann, grew up on the tales of Robin Hood. It was inevitable really, wasn't it? I am, of course, named Marion.

Where *were* those girls? Best do a quick check before I settled myself down somewhere.

Peering around me, I heard a yell. "Muuuuuuuum! Mum! Up here. On the walls." I looked up, squinting against the brilliance of the sun, wishing I had remembered to grab my sunglasses instead of leaving them, carelessly, on the table in the hall.

"Here, here!" A glimpse of scarlet caught my eye – Chloe's red tee shirt. Two pairs of hands were waving frantically at me from some kind of walkway at the top of the Abbey wall. I waved back and ambled off to find somewhere out of the way. It's funny, you would think red would be the worst colour to wear if you want to avoid bees but, from the research we've done, it seems to be a safer choice than blue or yellow. Of course, opinions vary, but from what I read, bees have trouble seeing the colour red. I hoped we were right.

I wandered around until I reached a small kind of hollow in the walls out of the way of the main tourist trails. Kicking my sandals off, I stretched out my feet blissfully against the grass. That was better. A nice cool, if rather unyielding, wall against my back and a good book. Now, I could have that peace and quiet I'd promised myself.

I was just getting into my book again when I realised there was a continuous buzzing in my head and...I sniffed...whatever was that? I looked to my left and saw a huge pile of canine excrement with its obligatory contingent of loudly buzzing flies.

Collecting my belongings hurriedly, I schlepped off down a grassy slope away from the Abbey. I could see an old tree down there on the right with a sort of fence around it. Plenty of shade there, and not a soul taking advantage of it. The girls wouldn't miss me for an hour or so.

The sun was hot on my head. Thinking longingly of my big, shady hat, which was lying next to my sunglasses on the hall table, I pulled the throw up to cover my head. I looked ridiculous, but it was better than getting sunstroke.

Heading towards the tree, I gradually became aware of another buzzing in my head. Not more flies, surely? No, it didn't sound like that, more like a swarm of bees. I looked upwards worriedly. If there were bees about, I needed to get back to Shannon fast.

But the skies were clear. The noise seemed to be coming from the tree itself, and there were no bees around that either. It echoed in my head, making me dizzy. It seemed to vibrate through my whole body. I could feel it in my fingers, my ribs, even my teeth. The grass shimmered, almost like a mirage. The sun was still beating down, but now I was covered in a cold sweat. My head spun, and I stumbled – I could hardly walk.

I tried to turn round and head back to the car, but I couldn't. Something seemed to be tugging me, almost as though there was a rope tied to me with someone hauling on the other end of it. I staggered forward. On and on, with a black mist dancing in my eyes, the buzz in my head engulfing me.

The tree was getting nearer and nearer. I felt so ill. If only I could just sit for a minute, but my unwilling feet kept moving forward, drawn by some irresistible force.

I felt sick and giddy, and I could hardly see, but I kept staggering towards that tree. The fencing around it seemed to have vanished, or maybe I'd found a gap; I didn't know, my eyes weren't focussing at all. Putting out a hand, I felt the gnarled trunk of the old beech, rough beneath my palm, before I pitched forward and fell into blackness.

CHAPTER TWO

Early May 1191

Etheldreda had been looking forward to harvesting the watercress needed for the infirmary potions and cures. The day was hot; the sun was high, and a trip to the stream outside the Abbey was in the nature of a treat. That was until Sister Ursel had told her who her companions were to be.

She sighed when told Sister Aldith was to accompany her. Aldith was barely out of the noviciate and thought she knew everything there was to know about being a fully-professed nun. Her pious demeanour seemed more of an act than true devotion, and she had an inclination to the dramatic.

"...for I am concerned about her attitude," said Sister Ursel. "And this is to go no further, mind." She gave Etheldreda a searching look and, seeing acquiescence there, continued. "True piety I mind not, but she is too young for this prideful piety of hers, and too ready to believe she has seen visions. That, in itself, would not be harmful, especially if God has blessed her with this gift – but if it is merely, as I suspect, the product of a fertile imagination, then it needs to be discouraged. An afternoon outside the Abbey, where there are none to impress, may help, I think."

Etheldreda nodded her understanding, but sighed inwardly. Sister Aldith, of all the other sisters, was not the one she would have chosen for company this bright day.

"And Brother Bernard has offered to accompany you."

Etheldreda's spirits sank a little further. Brother Bernard, who seemed to have the ability to make her feel like a lackwit!

"Now, look not so disappointed, Sister," chided Ursel, who was well-versed in reading faces. "Brother Bernard has a good heart and a helpful one, and it behoves us to see that Aldith gets a good dose of common sense. For she has a vocation, and who shall say her nay? Once we help her to overcome this youthful silliness, she will do well. Meantime, remember it is the Lord who gives us our joy, and by serving our brothers and sisters, that joy is increased, not diminished. Now, go find Aldith, and Brother Bernard will join you at the gatehouse."

Etheldreda had come late to the cloister. Married young to a man older and not of her choosing, who had nonetheless turned out to be a good husband to her, she had sincerely mourned him when he died but had no wish to be under a man's disposal again. When she arrived at Sparnstow Abbey, she had been welcomed into the fold along with her dowry, and once out of the noviciate, had been selected to work for Sister Ursel, the Abbey infirmaress, who also oversaw the small herbarium and the apothecary nuns. Ursel was a doughty soul, full of wisdom and compassion. Etheldreda had learnt much from her, and was hoping, one day, to become sub-infirmaress.

She pondered on Ursel's words as she approached Sister Aldith and, refusing to let anything steal her joy, advanced with a smile.

"Sister Aldith, come with me, if you please. Sister Ursel has a mission for us."

The young nun came reluctantly towards Etheldreda, speculation writ large on her face. Aldith was not at all sure what to make of Sister Ursel, who had yet to be impressed by her fine show of piety and was as like to dose her with some noxious tasting medicine when she was in a state of blessed ecstasy.

Sister Ursel was as far from appearing saintly to Aldith as anyone could be. Down-to-earth, and with a healthy scepticism, Aldith could not understand how the elderly infirmaress seemed to have the ear of Mother Abbess herself. And Etheldreda seemed to be cast in the same mould.

This was not how Aldith believed holy sisters should comport themselves.

Recollecting herself, Aldith lowered her eyes and, pressing her lips together in what she imagined to be a holy demeanour, she listened as Etheldreda told her what they would be doing.

Despite her determination to be kind, Etheldreda's heart sank as she watched the young nun veil her expression. *Ah, well.* Now, to the gatehouse to meet Brother Bernard. At least he had a kindly heart and a joyful countenance, for all his insistence that the Abbey sisters were weak vessels, needful to be assisted in all things. She really must learn to tolerate his determination to be helpful, and maybe he could bring some cheer back into the day.

Brother Bernard was waiting for them as they walked sedately to the gatehouse, baskets at his feet. Sister Berthe, the porteress, smiled benignly, her large face redder than usual today as she stood in the sunshine watching them depart.

Etheldreda and Aldith each carried one basket for the harvesting, Brother Bernard having two, one in either hand. They did not chatter but walked in companionable silence. It seemed to Etheldreda, when she glanced at her, that even Aldith was enjoying the day. She had forgotten to prim her mouth, and her eyes roved about her, taking in the beauty which surrounded them. In the distance, labourers worked the fields, calling to each other.

A golden sun burned brightly overhead, and the stream burbled and sang beside them, not quite drowning out the droning of bees and the birdsong. In an hour or so, it would be warmer, and even the birds would hush their singing. The day, so filled with promise, lay before her, and Etheldreda found her spirits rising again.

They crossed the bridge, and made their way to the place where the watercress grew in great profusion. Etheldreda slipped her sandals from her feet and prepared to kilt her habit slightly above her ankles.

Aldith's mouth turned down in disapproval. Brother Bernard noticed and gave a chuckle.

"Come, Sister, look not so sour at our good Sister Etheldreda, for she is in the right of it. Would you ruin good sandals by paddling in them? Here am I, removing mine also." And with that, he slipped his own large sandals from his sturdy feet and kilted his habit to his knees.

Thus admonished, Aldith had no choice but to follow suit, albeit with a sulky air. Crossing herself as though to ask pardon for committing some heinous sin, she bared her feet reluctantly.

"Now, Sister," Etheldreda instructed, "we will get splashed a little, but if we kilt our habits thus, not soaked. Brother Bernard will go into the deeper water, so we only need to raise our skirts barely above our ankles. It is no sin and needful for our task. Brother Bernard will avert his eyes."

She looked at Bernard, raising her eyebrows; he grinned and turned his back. He too, it appeared, found Aldith somewhat tiresome.

A scant while later, Etheldreda was delighted to see roses in Aldith's cheeks and a sparkle in her eyes. And after some strenuous work harvesting and a little more splashing in the stream than was strictly necessary, Aldith had seemed to find the time pass more pleasurably than Etheldreda thought she had first anticipated.

After much labour, Aldith placed a last handful of the watercress into her overflowing basket.

"Oof!" She stood upright and pressed a knuckle into her back as if to ease an aching muscle, but her eyes were lit with pleasure. For a pleasure it was, she had discovered, to be outside of the Abbey grounds on this fine day, and the water gurgling around her feet seemed to have seeped its way into her spirits.

Etheldreda smiled to see Aldith's enjoyment. Sister Ursel had been right to select her to accompany them. Splashing in the stream had quite banished the air of piety she liked to cultivate.

"You've worked well, Sister," she said approvingly. "Sister Infirmaress will be pleased. But see, our baskets are full. Come, it's time we returned."

"So soon?" The young nun's mouth turned downwards in disappointment.

"Aye, Sister Aldith. We've been at our labours long enough. We must get back to our other duties." Brother Bernard's back *was* aching, and he rumbled at Aldith like an old bear, but the twinkle in his eyes belied the frown in his voice.

"Come now, Sister, let us take this bounteous harvest back to our brethren and sisters."

One of the group of lay brethren who assisted the nuns at the insignificant Abbey of Sparnstow, Brother Bernard took his duties seriously, but, pernickety though he could be, he still seemed pleased to be here with the sisters, and it appeared he had, himself, enjoyed the day's labour. His job today had suited his nature, for as well as helping with their harvest of watercress, an escort was needful. Although they were permitted to leave the Abbey grounds for reasons such as this, it would be unseemly for the sisters to be unaccompanied.

Wading from the stream, he strode up the bank, his step firm and sure. The sun was so hot, his legs dried quickly, and he unkilted his habit which, despite his precautions, was damp about the hem. That, too, would dry soon enough.

"Come now. Give me your basket and then your hand, and let me help you back up the bank."

As Aldith took his hand, scrambling upwards with difficulty, Etheldreda took advantage of his distracted attention to climb nimbly back up the bank unaided. Truth to tell, she found his help somewhat patronising.

But there! I am being uncharitable again, she told herself sternly. And for sure, the toil had been pleasant enough in his company. For even he had seemed to shed some of his heavy officiousness, as well as his years, this past hour or two.

"Sister! What?" He frowned at her. "You did not wait for my aid?"

She smiled absently at him as he advanced towards her, holding out his hand for her basket, which she yielded willingly, and they plumped down on the grass, drying their feet with an old piece of sacking which Ursel had given Etheldreda. Replacing their sandals and taking up their baskets, they made ready to amble slowly back to the Abbey, each immersed in their own thoughts, enjoying the drowsy heat of the day, but passing the odd remark and, once, pointing out a kingfisher which suddenly dashed from a tree just by the water's edge.

As they crossed the small bridge, the companionable silence was rudely broken as Sister Aldith, who had been dallying and looking around her, let out a shriek of terror and fell to her knees, crossing herself wildly. Bernard and Etheldreda, turning in alarm, gaped at her. She looked as though she had, this time, indeed seen a vision.

Brother Bernard bent over her, putting his stout arm around her and lifting her, half fainting, to her feet. She gazed at them, her white face an exclamation of horror. Surely, no vision from the

Lord had brought this wild, staring look to her face. Bernard sat her down gently, and Etheldreda chafed her thin hands beneath her own sturdy, calloused ones.

"Whatever is wrong, child?"

Sister Aldith opened her mouth, but no sound came out. She raised her arm and pointed a shaking finger at the old beech which stood in a clearing not far from the stream. Their eyes followed her finger, at first seeing nothing.

"No! No!" Aldith gasped hoarsely. "Over there! A woman. On the grass. She fell…she fell…she fell out of the tree!"

"Out of the tree?" Brother Bernard scratched his head. "Well then, to be sure it might be strange that she was up in the tree, but…"

"No! No!" Aldith moaned. "She fell out of the trunk of the tree! Like some tree spirit. I am accursed. I am seeing demons." She buried her face in her hands, weeping.

"Oh, Aldith, Aldith, you have been out too long in the sun. You are overheated. It's my fault; I should have noticed. You shall lie down in the infirmary for a while. Come, let me help you." Sister Etheldreda was about to raise the shrinking young nun to her feet, when she heard a groan.

Brother Bernard lifted his head, gazing in the direction of the sound, which did, indeed, come from the beech tree.

He walked cautiously over to the tree and discovered the body of a woman, lying on the ground, partly hidden by the long grasses. Only half conscious, she was moaning and trying to lift herself. He put his hand to her shoulder, and she gazed at him uncomprehendingly. Bernard pushed her gently back to the ground. "Lie still, mistress, lie still."

CHAPTER THREE

I opened my eyes to see three worried faces peering at me. I couldn't think where I was for a moment. Oh! The Abbey. The heat. My head cleared, and I looked around me. Something was wrong.

Actually, my puzzled eyes were telling me that quite a lot was wrong. The buzzing in my head was fading slightly, and I could see now. At least, I thought I could, but nothing looked right. The tree seemed to be half the size of the one I remembered, and…and…I looked around, aghast.

Where was the car park? Where was the meadow? Come to that – no! The ruined Abbey was ruined no longer. It stood there, whole and proud in the afternoon sun. I blinked and pinched myself. It was still there. And these people! What were they wearing? *I must be dreaming.* I pinched myself again. It wasn't working. The ruins were still whole, and these three strange faces were still looking at me.

"Mistress, are you ailing?" the older of the two women asked me, concern in her bright blue eyes. The younger one appeared terrified of me and kept crossing herself.

"The ruins," I spluttered. "Where are they? Is this some kind of re-enactment?"

They looked at me with baffled faces. "Mistress, I fear you are indeed ailing," said the older woman. "I think...Aldith, do stop making the sign of the cross, Sister dear, you can see she is no spirit, but flesh and blood." She looked at the younger woman with an irritable frown then turned back to me. "I think we should bring you into the Abbey. You seem to be a little affected by the heat. Mayhap our infirmaress would be able to help. At the very least, you can rest awhile and perhaps drink a tisane."

Infirmaress? Tisane? But she seemed to want to help me, and I tried to collect my scattered wits. I must answer her, but decided I'd better say as little as possible until I knew what was happening. "Yes, I do feel rather odd. Maybe a – what did you call it – tisane?" I stumbled over the word. I had heard it before once or twice on holiday in France, but knew no one who actually used the expression, well, not in England anyway. "Maybe a drink would help. Thank you."

Maybe when I'd had a cup of whatever it was, I could get my head together and go find the girls.

They helped me gently to my feet, and I stumbled towards the building with them. We were only a few hundred yards from it, but I have never felt I have walked such a distance in my life as that strange walk.

I clutched my bag like a lifeline. Made of embroidered canvas, it held my last links to my life. But where was I now? In fact, it was beginning to dawn on me that I should question *when* rather than where. And how would I get back?

"Mistress, it would be usual to take visitors to our Abbess before anything else, but I think it best if we bring you to our infirmary first. You seem so dazed, and I think you may have hurt your head. Certainly, you might be suffering from the heat. It isn't to be taken lightly, my dear. I have seen it fell men as strong as oxen." The older nun smiled at me. The younger one looked on warily. "Brother, would you take the watercress in for us, then I think we have no more need of you. My thanks for your help."

The monk, for that was what he seemed to be, gave a gentle chuckle. "I'll warrant you were glad of my help today, Sister Etheldreda, with our tree maiden here. Like as not, without me you'd have had to manage both she and Sister Aldith, and that's more than enough for one sister, even you."

"Indeed." The nun, diminutive beside the huge monk, gave him a quelling look. "I do thank you, Brother, but I know you have duties elsewhere. Pray, do not let us keep you." He chuckled again and strode away.

"Oh dear. Mea culpa; I should not be so irritated by him, but he does think he is indispensable to those of us of the 'weaker sex,' still…" She sighed. "Now, Aldith, you are *not* to repeat that. Off you go, my dear. And take that frightened look off your face, you goose. You can see for yourself our visitor is no demon, just a poor soul who has addled wits from the heat and her fall. Hurry off, and say a prayer for her recovery now."

Aldith didn't appear to need telling twice. She turned and scuttled away like a frightened mouse which had just escaped from a cat.

Etheldreda turned to me. "A good girl," she murmured, "but far too imaginative. She sees omens and visions everywhere."

I just looked at her. Truly, I didn't know what to say.

"Don't worry," she soothed. "All will be well. We can trust our dear Lord for that."

I just hoped I could. It was slowly dawning on me that if I wasn't dreaming, and I had a horrible feeling I wasn't, then I was in real trouble.

I thought the best thing at the moment was to say nothing. I didn't really believe it; couldn't believe it, but everything was pointing to the fact that I seemed to be in some kind of different time. And although I wasn't great at history, I seemed to remember any women who were considered to be unusual were at risk of being condemned as witches. Heaven forbid I should put my foot in it here. I might never get home. And what about my girls? They would be worried to death. Thank God Chloe had her mobile. An involuntary gasp escaped me. *My mobile!* Presumably, it wouldn't work here, but if it did...I had a horrified vision of the effect it would have on these people if it should suddenly peal shrilly from my bag. We might be in an abbey, but all hell would be let loose. I needed to turn it off quickly, but I didn't want them to see it. I looked at, what was her name? Ah yes, Sister Etheldreda.

"I still feel a little faint. May I sit for a moment?"

"Yes, indeed. Whatever was I thinking of? Here." She led me to a small alcove with a bench. "Stay here, my dear, and I will fetch Sister Ursel, our infirmaress, to you. I will make haste. You rest."

I watched as she bustled out of sight, then I groped in my capacious bag. *Got it!* My head buried in my bag, trying to turn it off without being seen, I jumped when a hand was laid on my shoulder, nearly dropping the whole bag. My goodness! I must not let them see what it contained. In addition to my mobile, I had my satnav, a packet of aspirin, Shannon's epinephrine pen, my novel and a lot more stuff which would not be easy to explain; any of them might well look like witchcraft to these folk. I clutched it desperately to myself.

"Be easy, my dear." An elderly woman with a face like a wizened apple and twinkling hazel eyes was regarding me with humour. "I don't know what you have in your...er...sack," she paused, peering at it as though not sure she had the correct word, "but nobody here will be attempting to take it from you. This is God's house, my dear. You'll find no robbers here, and little surprises us. Come." She held out her hand and led me along shadowy corridors to the infirmary. The hard stone floor was cold to my feet, and I wondered what had become of my sandals.

Little surprises you, does it? I thought wryly. *I'll just bet I could spring a few shocks on you.*

We stepped inside a large room – a sort of ward, I suppose it was, with about ten wooden beds filled with people of varying ages, some with bandaged limbs, moaning, and one woman who had rough screens around her bed and sounded as though she might be in labour, plus some elderly women lying there, looking hopelessly at the ceiling. "Some of our residents are feeble-witted," Sister Ursel explained. "With no one else to care for them, we see them through their last days. Don't worry. They all have their own problems. Few of them will be interested in you." I looked at her worriedly, as she motioned to an empty bed. Why should she think I'd be worried they could hear me? What did she think of me? Maybe it was just me. Maybe her words were normal, just meant to be reassuring. Yes, that would be it. I had enough to stress about, without seeing problems where there were none.

"Now, let me see." She laid a cool hand on my forehead, peered into my eyes, then took my hand. As she lifted it, she started and paused for a moment, staring hard at my fingers. A frown puckered her wrinkled brow even more than it already was. She gazed deeply into my eyes again and, taking the shawl from my head and shoulders, looked at my upper arms. She gasped and draped the shawl back around me. "Just stay here. Don't move. Don't take that shawl off, and whatever you do, do *not* let anyone look into your bag."

She hurried off, almost running. I had no idea such an elderly woman could move so fast.

I sat there, gazing around me. Despite my fears and confusion, I couldn't help but try to take it all in. It was like a living history lesson. I was puzzled over one thing though – well, I say one thing, but everything was a puzzle. However, it seemed curious to me that I could understand the speech of these people. I might be wrong, but I thought that the kind of English or French, or whatever they spoke back in medieval times, was supposed to be nothing like the language spoken in my own time. Yet, apart from some slightly odd turns of phrase, I had no trouble understanding these people, and they me. It was odd. Maybe I was wrong. I shrugged. I had more important things to worry about.

A touch on my hand brought me back to my surroundings. The infirmaress was back with a tall, aristocratic-looking nun. This must be the Abbess. About fifty years old with an aquiline nose and high cheekbones, we could have been in the presence of royalty. I almost felt an urge to curtsey.

She stopped in front of me and studied me, taking my tanned left hand in her slim white one, saying almost under her breath, "Hmm. Yes, I see. And you say she has the mark? Very well."

She looked into my eyes. "You're very far from home, my dear. Don't speak. Just follow me."

Trailing through the cloisters behind her, I was becoming even more alarmed. All I wanted to do was run back to the old tree and see if I could return to my own time. As the thought crossed my mind, she opened a door into a small but comfortably furnished room. Not opulent but definitely not what I had expected a nun's cell to be. But then, she was the Abbess. I supposed she had a little more luxury than the average nun. Probably came with the territory.

"Please enter, my child. Don't even think about what is in your mind. It won't work, you know. Not yet."

I gaped. Could she read my thoughts?

"No, child. There is no witchcraft here. I cannot read your thoughts."

Oh yeah? She was doing a good job of that so far.

"Sit." She indicated a chair beside a large, carved wooden desk.

"Now, child, I am the Abbess Hildegarde. Won't you tell me your name and your time?"

"My age?"

"No, child, your *time*. From *when* do you come?"

I gasped. "You know?" I felt a glimmer of hope rising.

She smiled. "I do, indeed."

"My name is Marion."

The Abbess seemed to freeze for a second, then peered closely at my face, a frown on her own as she gazed at me. I was beginning to feel very uncomfortable, when suddenly, her face cleared. She sat back in her chair and smiled.

"How strange life can be," she murmured, looking down, then raising her gaze back to mine. "You have a family?" She indicated my wedding and engagement rings.

"Yes, my husband and I have two children. Chl...Eleanor and Rohese." I thought I'd better not say Chloe and Shannon.

She nodded in approval. "Very well done, child. Now, what are their real names? Tell no one but me, but I should like to know."

"Chloe and Shannon."

"Very pretty, but not from my time. Far nicer than my own."

Big tears started to well up in my eyes. "I don't know how to get back to them." With that, the enormity of maybe never seeing them again hit me fully. I put my head on the desk and wailed.

She came around the desk and put her arm about me, raising my head, looking into my eyes. "Marion, don't fret, all will be well. You will see them again, I promise."

Someone tapped on the door. Sister Ursel entered, bearing a steaming mug, or I suppose I should call it a tankard, maybe. It looked like a mug to me, anyway. The Abbess took it from her and waved her away, carefully locking the door behind her.

"Drink this, Marion. It isn't tea, I know, but you'll find it quite pleasant and very comforting."

I gaped at her. "You know about tea?"

She threw her head back and pealed with very un-nun-like laughter.

"Marion, I adore tea. And I haven't tasted it for nigh on thirty years. At first, I wondered how I would ever survive without it. But as you see, here I am."

"You know? How? And how do you know about my time?"

She took my hands. "Your rings, my dear. They are twentieth century, yes? Nothing like that is made in this age. Your rings are from the future."

"But how do you *know* these things?"

"There is another clue," she said, pointing at my shawl. "May I take this?"

I clutched it to myself nervously. "Sister Ursel said not to remove it."

"Ah, yes, but you needn't worry about me. That's why she fetched me, you see."

She gently peeled the shawl from my shoulders and pointed to my vaccination mark. Then, she rolled up the sleeve of her habit and showed me her own arm. Sure enough, dimpling the skin was a small round scar. "Safest not to let anyone see that. It may be taken for a witch's mark," she said seriously.

I sat there stunned and gawping. This tall abbess – from my time? I couldn't believe it.

"Surely you don't think you are the only one who has ever wandered too close to that old tree? I was in my twenties, studying to be a doctor. They needed me here. It only ever brings people through when there's a need."

"But you're still *here*," I wailed. "You didn't get back. How do you know I will?"

"I chose to stay. They needed me so. It was meant to be, child. We must need you for some purpose yet to be unravelled, then you may choose to stay or go. But you have no choice, truthfully. I had no family. You belong with your family. You will return to them, but for now, you are here. You may as well enjoy the time; when it is right, you will get back." She looked at me calmly. "Now, we just have to find out why you're here, and what to do with you until we know. For now, we'll have to pretend you've need of shelter and we've taken you in, maybe as a lay sister. It's all right." She laughed at my horrified expression. "You won't have to be a nun, just help out a little. Stand up, Marion, dear, let me take a closer look at you."

I stood obediently, and she walked around me, tapping her chin with her finger, deep in thought. "Hmm. Yes, the timing has worked very well. There have been others…"

"Others?" I spluttered.

"Well, of course, dear, but only a very few. And some of them have been quite unsuitably dressed. It has been very difficult to explain them away. But you, Marion, unless anyone were to look too closely, blend in fairly well. Is that the style these days? Very nice. Comfortable, too, I should imagine. Of course, the top is nowhere near modest enough, but if we keep that nice shawl wrapped around you…" She put her head on one side, considering. "Yes, if we wrap it just so, I think it will do."

She tugged gently at the waistband of my dress. "Ah, elastic. Yes, I remember it. Wonderful stuff. Now, we don't know how long you're here for, but I think we may need to hide that and your underwear if you're still here tonight." She paused for a moment. "I suppose it can be concealed beneath a shift."

"My underwear?"

"Oh yes. Elastic?" I nodded. "Bra? Panties? Slip? Nobody wears anything like that in these times. Still, let's see. You may not be here long enough to worry about that. Just do as Sister Ursel instructed and keep that shawl tied tightly over your top. Also keep your head covered with it. Your hairstyle, you know, would be remarked on."

"Sister Ursel knows?" What was it with these time-travelling nuns?

Abbess Hildegard looked at me indulgently. "Well, I had to explain my knowledge of healing to someone. Ursel is older than I and knows how to keep secrets. She is widely recognised as a healer in these parts. That's due in no little wise to what I taught her added to the skills she already had. Ursel won't tell. And she is teaching Sister Etheldreda. That girl is very quick to work things out. I shall bring her into the secret if need be, but for now, the fewer who know, the better."

I sat down again, still feeling rather shaky, and took a cautious sip of whatever it was Sister Ursel had brought me. It actually tasted quite pleasant. I think it may have had some wine in it, certainly some herbs and honey. It was like nothing I had tasted before but, yes, it really was rather nice. I sipped some more. Hildegarde smiled approvingly.

"That's right, drink it up. It will do you good."

We sat there quietly for a few moments as I drank. She was right. It did seem to help calm me a little. My heart didn't seem to be pounding quite so hard and the trembling inside me had eased.

My mug drained, the Abbess became serious. "Now, to business. Would you mind if I had a look in that bag of yours? I may replace it with a basket, I think. It's quite ornate. It will be provoking rumours of theft or something. Do you mind?"

I held it out obediently, and she rummaged inside.

"What in the world is this?" She held out my mobile phone.

"Abbess, if you don't mind me asking, when *was* your time?"

"The nineteen-seventies. I used to be called Doreen." She sighed reminiscently. "It was quite a good time. We did have some wonderful music. Sometimes, one wearies of all this chanting. But there! It is a small price to pay. I just thank the good Lord I wasn't wearing a mini or bell-bottoms when I fell through. That would have caused quite a commotion. Happily, I'd opted to wear a maxi dress that day. It didn't quite fit this era, but it caused considerably less confusion than the other options. Wearing those, I don't know what would have happened to me. Can you imagine their faces?" She threw back her head, and the room rang with a peal of such merriment. I liked this woman.

"So what is it?" She fiddled with it, pressing the buttons.

I took it from her quickly before she could switch it on. "It's a way of communicating. It's a phone, but not like you would have known."

"Ah, I see." She nodded. "Like a walkie-talkie?"

"Something like that."

She rummaged again and held out my satnav.

"Now, that is a way of finding your directions when driving. It talks to you."

Her eyes sparkled with amusement. "It does? And men actually listen? In my day, they never took directions from anyone."

"Not much has changed there, then. They listen to technology, but they still don't listen to their wives." I grinned, remembering the many times Tom hadn't followed my directions and had got himself lost.

Suddenly, there was a commotion outside and a peremptory hammering upon the door. Abbess Hildegarde opened it hurriedly to find a group of men, her indignant porteress standing flushed and furious beside them, arms akimbo.

"Sister Berthe?" Hildegarde raised an enquiring eyebrow.

One of the men started to speak at the same time as Sister Berthe squawked indignantly, "Mother Abbess, they refused to remove their swords. I've told them they can't come into the Abbey armed!"

As Berthe spluttered in indignation, the man, evidently the spokesman of the group, glared at her murderously. He was tall with a neatly trimmed black beard and a hawkish face, lean and well-muscled. He looked capable of cruelty but at the moment was showing signs of strain. Turning on the porteress, he swore violently. "Shut your mouth, crone." The other men crowded behind him all talking at once.

"Silence!" Hildegarde held up her hand, and they ceased immediately. There was something to be said for authority here. "Sister Berthe? What is happening? Why this disturbance?"

As Sister Berthe opened her mouth to speak, the black-bearded man clamped an arm around her, holding his hand against her mouth. Hildegarde's eyes blazed with fury. "I apologise for silencing this clucking old hen." Berthe's eyes bulged with anger against his muffling hand. "But our need is most urgent, Abbess. Will, bring Jo...er, Jankin forward please."

A fair-haired young giant and another man lifted a sort of stretcher before the Abbess. On it lay a greatly distressed, elegantly dressed man in his early to mid-twenties, with a graze on his head, his face bloated, eyes swollen shut, and a tinge of blue beginning to form around his mouth. He gasped for breath, his chest making a distressing noise.

"Abbess, we need your infirmaress urgently but not in the infirmary. Have you a private chamber?"

Hildegarde seemed to sum up the situation in a heartbeat. "Follow me, and Sister Felicia," to a nun who, hearing the clamour, had run to them, eyes wide with fear, "fetch Sister Ursel! *Run!*" She snapped her fingers at the young nun, who turned and fled through the cloisters, her veil streaming behind her like a large bird.

Their spokesman indicated the man on the stretcher. "It's Jankin, here. We don't know what's happened to him. One moment all was well; the next, he fell from his horse. He had hit his head a short while earlier but, apart from this graze, it did not seem to cause him serious hurt. He appeared well enough after. And look! See his face. What ails him, Abbess? Can you do aught for him?"

The Abbess looked closely at him, then straightened, a grave look on her face. "I'm not sure. We shall see what we can do. Please, come with me." She set off through the cloisters, the men following her.

I stood there for a moment, then grabbed my bag and went after them. I'd seen this before.

Abbess Hildegarde opened the door to a large, well-furnished chamber as Sister Ursel came bustling to meet them. The men laid Jankin tenderly on the bed, and Ursel bent to examine him, then stood, a look of worry on her face. "He hit his head, did he? Yet, this is not caused by a head wound. I've only seen it once before. Has something stung him, do you know?"

Their leader scratched his chin and looked thoughtful. "Stung? Why yes, a while ago. But–"

Ursel interrupted, "Wasp or bee?"

"I forget. Is it of great matter? Anyone else see it, lads?"

There was a general shuffling, but none of them spoke up.

"Oh, get out of my way. Men! Useless great knaves," she muttered under her breath, as she removed his mantle. "Now, help me get his tunic off."

They carefully did her bidding, easing it off him as gently as they could.

Ursel examined him, unlacing the neck of his shirt. "Yes, here is the sting. Here is the bee too, look." A dead bee fell from just inside his shirt, tumbling onto the bed beside its victim. "Now, I need to get rid of this sting. And I need to think. Out! Out!" She clapped her hands and drove the men from the room, then gently eased out the sting, being careful to avoid getting more poison into her patient's ailing body.

Hildegarde looked at her gravely. "Can you do anything?"

"Mayhap, but the last person I saw taken like this died. Nothing I could do."

I stepped into the gap between them, speaking in low tones. "I think I might be able to help. At least, I can try. But you need to keep them out." I nodded at the men, who were still milling anxiously in the doorway.

"Out, gentlemen. Out! Out! Out!" Hildegarde clapped her hands at them as though they were recalcitrant infants. Taken by surprise, they stepped backwards involuntarily. Hildegarde shut the door and dropped the sneck into place.

I feverishly rummaged in my bag for Shannon's spare adrenaline. It had to be there. Why couldn't I find it? *Calm down and start again*, I told myself. Slowing my scrabbling hands down, I forced myself to go methodically through my bag. There it was. Gasping with relief, I grabbed it. "Sit him up," I instructed. Ursel looked bewildered. "Just do it."

They didn't argue but got behind him and raised him to an upright position. I held the epinephrine pen in my fist, swung my arm and jabbed him in the thigh with it.

Hildegarde and Ursel stood there staring, their mouths perfect Os of astonishment.

Holding my breath, I gently rubbed the injection site until the swelling started to go down. It probably took less than three minutes, but it felt like an hour. That awful rasping noise he'd been making eased. He really needed to have proper medical attention, but I couldn't very well take him back to the tree and disappear with him. I had to hope he would be okay. "That's all I can do, the rest is up to God. It may work. If not…" I shrugged.

Abbess Hildegarde looked around, then thrust my bag at me. "Put that away quickly," she muttered, striding to the door. "God be praised, gentlemen, we have a miracle. He is recovering. I'll leave you with Sister Ursel." She turned to me, "Marion, with me now, if you please."

I didn't need telling twice. I clutched my bag to me, scrunching it up as tightly as I could so they didn't get much of a look at it. We had not got as far as transferring my belongings to the basket Hildegarde had produced.

I needn't have bothered. No one noticed me. All eyes were on Jankin as they surged into the chamber behind us.

"Sister Etheldreda." Hildegarde gestured to the nun I'd seen previously, who was coming towards the infirmary. "Walk with me." They spoke quietly together as they headed for Hildegarde's chamber, with me scurrying behind. As we reached the door, Etheldreda hurried off. The Abbess almost pushed me into her room and closed the door.

"Quickly, we haven't much time. Tell me all you know about what happened. This seems to be an allergic reaction. I haven't seen one, but the symptoms seem to indicate that."

I nodded. "Yes, it seems he is allergic to bee stings. If it happens again he probably will die without this." I held up the epinephrine. Hildegarde took it from me and examined it.

"Hmm. I seem to remember hearing about this. It was still in the research stage back then, I think. Certainly, I've never seen one. There's a use-by date on the side." She studied it and grinned. "July 2006. I don't think that will help much, will it? Might it last a little longer, though?" She considered, head on one side, eyes creased in thought."

I took it from her gently. "Abbess, it only lasts for one injection. You cannot use it twice."

She sighed. "I thought it was too good to be true. I've learnt much about herbs since I've been here. Unfortunately, I have yet to find a herb which might do anything similar to this. Never mind. The most important thing at the moment is what to do about you. There's no time to waste and no time to explain, but I very much fear your presence here has put you in grave danger."

A sudden scratching at the door made me jump. Etheldreda came in with a bundle. The Abbess took it from her and turned to me.

"Quick. No time to waste. Take off your dress and put this on." She thrust a habit into my hands. "I'll take care of your gown." Hildegarde took my dress as I stepped out of it and gave it to Etheldreda, who left the room quietly. Hildegarde helped me into the unfamiliar garb of a nun, fingers flying as she fastened it around me.

"Now, in here. Make haste!" She pushed aside a cupboard, revealing a hidden door which she opened, motioning me to step inside. I found myself in a small, dark cell. "It used to be a punishment cell a long time ago. Not many people remember it now. Stay still, and whatever you do, don't make any noise!" She kindled a small horn lantern, pushed it into my hands and shut the door hurriedly. I was left alone in the dark.

I hate confined spaces, and I'm not over fond of the dark either. I don't mind it too much as long as it isn't pitch black, but the darkness inside this cell was inky, apart from the small circle illuminated by my lamp. I couldn't see anything beyond the area just around me.

Holding out my lamp, I tried to penetrate the heavy darkness which seemed to press against my eyes. To my right, I could make out a wall. I took a careless step forward and banged my shin on something low to the ground. Holding the lantern lower, I found some kind of bed with a mattress stuffed with straw or something. I sat gingerly, hoping there were no bugs in it. Raising my lantern, I tried to make out more of the room, but the light was so dim, I gave up.

Sitting there, afraid to move in case I made a noise, I tried to quell the tide of panic welling up in me. The blackness was so thick it seemed to threaten to extinguish my small glimmer of light. Terrified in case it went out, I concentrated on the space in front of me which I knew to be the door. If I looked really hard, I imagined I could see a thin sliver of light coming from the edge. I kept my eyes on that and stayed there, still, mute with fear.

A commotion in the room beyond made me jump. Loud voices, clanking weapons, and then Hildegarde's calm voice. "Please be seated, gentlemen. What can I do for you?"

A harsh voice – the spokesman, the one I had noticed. "Abbess, do you know who J...Jankin is?"

"I am not sure. Will you tell me?"

"Safer you know nothing. And safer by far if you forget anything you've seen today."

Hildegarde's voice showed no trace of fear.

"How can I forget something which never happened to someone I have never met?"

"And what of your women? The sisters?"

"Most of my sisters have seen nothing. They are sheltered young women; indeed, they rarely leave the confines of the Abbey. You have nothing to fear from their tongues, my lord."

"What about the old one. The infirmaress? She saw everything."

"My lord, we are nuns, women of God. We do not gossip. We do not involve ourselves with worldly things. We are here to serve the Lord. We pray; we nurse; we work. We do little else. We mix little with those from the outside."

"Very well, so be it. Be sure your daughter nuns do not remember anything they have seen. Now, about the young woman who entered the infirmary with you."

I felt myself go cold. An involuntary shiver ran through me at the menace in the voice.

"Ah, yes. She was merely here delivering a message. She has gone now. She saw very little." The calm voice was assured. "I believe she lives some way off, and I am very sure she understood nothing of what she saw."

Part of me was shocked. This woman was an abbess. Yet I supposed she was telling a version of the truth.

"So you say, Abbess, but I think it behoves us to make sure of that. And before we go, I think we will just take a look around to make sure she didn't linger. One of my men will remain with you while we search."

"As you wish." The Abbess sounded cold and disapproving. "Do *not* accost my nuns. You will treat them with the respect which should be accorded to holy sisters. And don't frighten them. Some of them are of a nervous disposition and not used to men. I think I shall accompany you."

The sound of heavy footsteps receded.

CHAPTER FOUR

Etheldreda looked about her. The dark-faced man, the one who seemed to be in control, glanced in her direction and beckoned her over. She stood meekly before him and lowered her eyes.

"Look at me, woman! Have you seen any of us before?"

"No, my lord." Her heart hammered so hard she could barely speak.

"Good. You would do well never to see us again. In truth, you would do better to never have seen us at all."

"I shall endeavour to forget you have ever been here, my lord."

"See that you do." He tilted her chin upward with an iron grip. "You are very composed, Sister. Do you not fear me?"

"Sire, I believe that my Lord will protect me. I know you could crush me like an ant, but would you not fear for your mortal soul to harm a bride of Christ? We have no interest in worldly things. We are here only to serve our Lord." Some mischief prompted her to add, "You need have no fear of *us*."

She nearly choked. Where had she found the courage – or was it foolhardiness – to say such a thing? She stole a glimpse at his face. His lips were twitching. Thank God, he seemed to be more amused than angry.

"Well, I'm thankful for that, lass," he spluttered. "What a weight off my mind. Now, off with you. Be about your business."

Etheldreda needed no further encouragement. Thank goodness he hadn't asked to see inside her basket.

"Wait!" He was staring at her. She held her breath. "Keep me in your prayers, Sister."

She nodded, not daring to pause longer, and walked briskly away, still holding her breath until she had moved out of sight around a corner. The Abbess and their strange visitor were depending on her.

Trying to move calmly and not attract attention, she looked neither to the right nor left, ignoring the men who surged about, so out of place in the Abbey grounds. At last, she reached the gatehouse.

Sister Berthe was more than usually abrupt. The day's events had unsettled her, and being manhandled by that great churl had upset her dignity. The sight of those knaves befouling her beloved Abbey with their raucous voices and irreverent remarks had roused her temper to something quite unsuited to her calling, and she was struggling to overcome the rising tide of fury which threatened to burst from her in an unseemly display of anger.

Taking a deep breath, Berthe tried to calm herself. She must not take out her ire on her sisters. She fixed a determined smile on her face. "Sister Etheldreda, what might you be wanting?"

Etheldreda dipped her head respectfully. "Sister Berthe, the Abbess has requested me to do an errand for her. I pray you, give me leave."

"Humph!" Berthe tutted and fussed as she opened the gates. "Well, 'tis most irregular. Knows she that you are unaccompanied? That isn't in our rule, indeed 'tisn't." Disapproval was clear on her large florid face.

"Mother Abbess knows this but has need of me to act for her. It is a matter of the utmost secrecy. She asks you to hold silence; to tell no one. But the need is most urgent." Etheldreda didn't want to raise Berthe's curiosity, but she had to tell the porteress something, although she knew Mother Abbess wanted her to say as little as possible. However, mercifully, at that moment, one of the men-at-arms left on guard in the grounds decided it would be good sport to throw stones at Horace, the old nag who lived in the stables. The horse shied in alarm, rolling his eyes until the whites showed. Berthe, a grim look on her face, dismissed Etheldreda with a wave of her hand.

Huffing, she shut the gate behind her. "Well now, Sister, take care and be back as soon as possible. Tsk. Most irregular."

Having performed her duty, Berthe swept over to stand protectively before Horace, telling his tormentor exactly what she thought of men who persecuted harmless beasts.

Etheldreda sagged with relief and went on her way before Sister Berthe could return to ask more questions.

She felt a flutter of excitement alongside the frisson of fear. It was rare that she was outside of the Abbey at this time of day and never alone, but there was no time to waste. She may have amused the knight who had spoken to her, but she had little doubt that he would not treat her well if he were to discover her errand. Etheldreda had sensed he would be capable of cruelty if roused. She moved smartly out of sight of the Abbey and looked for a suitable place. Yes, this would do. No one in sight. She stepped into the cover of a small copse and pulled out the contents of the basket.

Safely hidden from view, she hesitated a moment – it felt so strange to be disrobing here. She crossed herself and uttered a prayer, before quickly removing her outer garment. For a moment she stood there, gazing at the gown she held, wondering at how stretchy it was. What fabric was this? She tugged the outlandish thing over her head, pulling it down around her hips and smoothing it as best she could.

It felt so light, so comfortable. But the garment didn't even fully cover her shift. To expose herself thus felt shocking. What manner of woman dressed like this? Surely she was not…*No, of course not*. She must trust her Abbess and do as she was bid. At least she had the shawl to cover herself with. Swiftly she pulled off her wimple and veil. She stood there for a moment, enjoying the nearly forgotten feel of the sun on her cropped head, then recollecting her position, wrapped the shawl around her and secured it firmly about herself. Now she felt less bare, a little more seemly, but oh, she had never understood how comforting her habit was until this moment. She folded it neatly, hiding it beneath a cloth. Ensuring her head and shoulders were completely covered, Etheldreda gritted her teeth and headed towards the village.

On such a day as this, it would have been nice to dawdle, but she must be getting on. She needed to be seen, but not by the men at the Abbey. The knight who had spoken to her may have been amused by her boldness, but if caught on this errand, it was likely he'd not be merciful. He had the face of one who was unused to being thwarted.

She walked quickly across the bridge straddling the stream, then ran lightly towards the village.

"Make certain you are seen," the Abbess had instructed her, "but don't let them see your face, don't speak and don't look anyone in the eye."

It was an easy deception if she was observed from a short distance, for she was a similar build and age to Marion, but their faces were not at all alike. Marion's was slim and pale with dark brows and brown eyes; Etheldreda's was round and rosy with pale brows and eyes the colour of forget-me-nots. If any of the villagers described her face when questioned, as she knew they would be, there would be no hope of deceiving the knight, and it would go badly for the Abbess, maybe for Etheldreda herself. Who knew what the repercussions would be? Etheldreda didn't understand exactly what was happening, but she knew there was danger here. Crossing herself and saying a quick prayer as she approached the first few houses in the village, she slowed. Good. She could see plenty of folk going about their business. It was a reasonably large village with several alehouses, but people always notice strangers – outsiders; it is human nature, and in this well-made garment in soft shades of green, she would be sure to attract their attention.

She walked briskly through the village, looking straight ahead, resisting the temptation to gaze about her. A huge man, with arms like tree trunks, crossed her path and stared curiously at her. Her heart beat so loud, she thought it would burst from her breast. Head down, she stared at the ground and swerved around him. He put a hand out and caught at her shawl. Ripping it from him, she took to her heels and fled as though the hounds of hell were on her heels. He stood gawking after her.

"I were only goin' to ask 'er if she wanted to share an ale wi' me," he complained to the alewife who stood there, arms akimbo, glaring at him. "She 'ad no cause to run off like that. I weren't goin' to do 'er no 'arm, an' thass the truth." The alewife rolled her eyes and returned to her alehouse.

Etheldreda ran until she judged a safe distance was between her and the villager. In truth, she could not have run further. Convent life had not equipped her for this sort of exercise. Panting, she held her free hand to her side. A stitch ripped mercilessly through her, and a pulse in her neck throbbed, tightening about her throat like a band of iron, until she could barely breathe.

Winded, she leant against a tree, until she realised she was attracting more attention than was wise. A stout woman was heading in her direction, concern on her face. Etheldreda gathered what was left of her disordered senses, took one more deep breath and, turning her head away from the anxious woman, made determinedly for the outskirts of the village. Behind her, she knew people were watching her and shaking their heads. Ah well, at least she would not be easily forgotten.

Legs trembling beneath her skirts, she disappeared into the trees, praying she would not be followed.

Once hidden from sight, she paused, looking around her in trepidation. Had she any pursuers? It seemed not. Not a sound came from behind her. Sweat ran down her back, and her breathing came in ragged gasps. At last, though, she could rest for a few moments and recover. She found a tree stump and sat down shakily.

Etheldreda dared not enter too deeply into the woods, it would not be safe for a woman alone, and yet she must be far enough in to be well hidden from view. This was probably sufficient distance. Watching and listening, she removed Marion's clothing and dived back into her own, relieved to be enveloped in the safe and familiar habit again. Once more recognisable as a nun, she felt a little less afraid. She replaced her own head coverings, tucking the gown and shawl, which would give her deception away if they should be discovered, deep into her basket and covering them with the cloth. Then, looking about her for the herbs she had been instructed to return with, she bent to her task, throwing them on top of the cloth with unsteady hands.

Suddenly, she heard something crashing through the woods behind her. She turned in alarm and froze in terror as she found herself looking into the face of an angry boar. He stood just yards from her, squealing with rage; piggy eyes filled with fury. For a moment, black specks danced dizzyingly in her vision.

Anchored to the spot, she tried to think. The tusks of a boar were lethal. One false move and she would be skewered. Unable to move an inch, limbs quivering, she could do nothing but pray. Although afraid to take her gaze from its face, Etheldreda forced herself to close her eyes and commune with the One whom she trusted above all. Slowly, warmth flooded through her, her legs stopped trembling and a calm came over her. What would be, would be. Opening her eyes, she found she was alone in the forest. The beast had gone.

She knelt, awed, for a few moments of prayer and thanksgiving, her heart full of gratitude, before resuming her task. Soon the herbs were bulging from her basket, covering its dangerous contents completely. Tidying herself and brushing leaves from her habit, she left the forest further down the track than she had entered, this time skirting around the village. A small hill hid her from sight as she returned to the Abbey, this time calmly, with a measured tread, once again one of the holy sisters of Mother Church, as unlike the mysterious, fleet-footed woman who had sped through the village an hour previously as could be imagined.

CHAPTER FIVE

Sister Ursel had seen surprisingly rapid improvement in the man his friends called Jankin. Saturnine of face, he had nevertheless been capable of great charm once he had returned to his senses.

The elderly nun had been quite won over, blushing as he called her his 'Goodwife Nurse,' and chuckling at his nonsense as he soundly kissed her on both wrinkled cheeks. His companions showed less charm, brusquely barging their way around the chamber and insisting he leave as soon as he was able. Dismissing them with a flick of his fingers, he stood up on now-steady legs and made a graceful obeisance to the Abbess.

"My thanks, good ladies." He smiled, and Ursel looked as though the sun had come out.

"You are most welcome, Sire. We are delighted to see you so improved in health." Hildegarde was speaking the truth. Less easily impressed than Ursel, she sensed petulance behind the gracious manners and a temper which would be quick to burn and slow to fade. She suspected their patient's true identity, although clearly his men were attempting to pass him off as merely a friend of theirs. This was a very dangerous young man, she had no doubt of that. She would be relieved when he and his companions had shaken the dust of the Abbey from their feet and returned to whence they had come.

He smiled at her and shook his head. "Oh, faithless one, you do not trust me." He flashed his brilliant smile at her again. Then, his mouth turned suddenly down and a dark cloud shadowed his eyes. "Well, and mayhap you are wise. Sometimes, I fear for my very soul. But I promise you this, my lady Abbess, I will not forget the faithful service you and these gentle sisters have rendered to me this day. You will find I am grateful to those who give me reason. As is my lady mother. You shall be recompensed. No." He wagged his finger at her as she opened her mouth to remonstrate. "Do not say me nay. Give me this chance to redeem my soul."

"Sire, we are ever at your service." Hildegarde bowed her head slightly. "But I believe your companions are restless to be on their way. Go with God, my lord. We will keep you in our prayers."

He bowed again. "I thank you, my lady Abbess," he said, giving her a wry look. "I fear I have need of much prayer." He left the room with a slight swagger. As he turned to his men, the arrogance returned to his face. "Well, de Soutenay, you have your way as usual. Come." He swept from the cloister without a backward glance.

"But my lord," de Soutenay said, striding behind him, "we have not yet found the young woman."

"De Soutenay, your men have searched the Abbey from top to bottom. Either they are ineffective, or she is not here. No matter, she won't have got far, we shall ask in the village. She sounds like a wood nymph. Most intriguing. I fancy a glimpse of this nymph myself; I feel sure someone must have seen her. Let us waste no more time." He swung onto his horse, raised one hand in a careless salute to the Abbess, and, to her great relief, the entire troop mounted and left. She would have been less relieved had she heard his next conversation.

As they rode away, Sister Ursel turned towards Hildegarde, a look of worry replacing the twinkle she had obliged their erstwhile patient with. "Mother Abbess," she murmured, looking discreetly around her, "I'm very much afraid Sister Aldith has been gossiping. He asked about our 'wood nymph', as he called her."

Hildegarde pursed her lips. A frown creased her brow. "Aldith?"

"Yes, Mother Abbess. She was with Sister Etheldreda when they came upon Marion. She was much disturbed; you know how given to flights of fancy she is."

"Why does this not surprise me?" Although Aldith was now a fully-professed nun, she had yet to learn to school her tongue and was inclined to the dramatic; Hildegarde was well aware of her tendency to find visions and demons in any and every situation. In most of the other sisters, she would have considered the possibility of divine blessing, but of Aldith's visions she had a lurking suspicion, it having been necessary to speak to her severely on more than one occasion about her manner. She listened to Ursel with growing concern. This could have serious repercussions.

"Etheldreda mentioned that Aldith feared Marion to be a demon or spirit. Unfortunately, it appears that she did see something of her entrance. Etheldreda thought she had dealt with her, but–"

"Sister Ursel, you surely did not allow her to serve Lord John? For you did know he was John of Mortain, did you not?" She regarded Ursel gravely.

"Of course I kept her from him, for like you, I recognised him. I kept his door tight shut, but I caught her gossiping with Sister Jovetta just outside his chamber. I admonished her severely about the sins of gossip and spreading false report and reminded her that holy sisters should have still tongues, but I'm very much afraid the damage has been done."

"I will deal with Aldith myself, but not until this has been resolved. That tongue of hers *must* be brought under control." Hildegarde looked at the worried nun beside her with compassion, laying a hand on her arm. "Never fret, Sister Ursel. We must pray we can get Marion back to where she came and that, right speedily. Be easy, we shall leave it with our Lord."

"Easy to say," grumbled the old lady, earning herself a reproachful gaze, "but that hell-bound spawn – forgive me, Mother Abbess – will not easily forget what he heard." She crossed herself reflectively.

"Why, Sister!" Hildegarde was surprised. "I had thought you were rather taken with him."

"Aye, and I'll warrant so did he." Ursel's lips twitched. "'Goodwife Nurse' indeed. Pshaw! I may be old, but I'm not so simple as to not know when I'm being taken for a fool. Two may play that game."

She turned to go, then looked back at Hildegarde, concern on her face. "It may be a sin, but I do admit I'm worried. We will be able to do it, won't we, Mother? Get her back safely?"

"I believe so. We will pray for guidance, and for John's soul," Hildegarde added, feeling guilty that it had been an afterthought.

"Oh! As to that," Ursel muttered as she turned away again, "that *would* be a miracle, an' all, that would." She stomped off towards the infirmary.

Hildegarde watched the elderly nun thoughtfully. Ursel had fooled her, certainly. It would seem likely John had swallowed it too, the wily old besom. How to allay her fears now?

"Is anything too hard for God, Sister?" Her clear voice challenged Ursel, ringing through the air.

"Nay, but they do say the devil looks after his own," grumbled Ursel to herself without turning back. She spied Sister Aldith walking across the grounds, as innocent-looking as a new-born babe, and smiled grimly. Cleansing and bandaging old Sister Godleva's badly ulcerated legs for a week or two would give her a chance to reflect upon the evils of gossip. Calling, "Sister Aldith, wait," she hastened towards her. Retribution was about to fall upon the head of the unsuspecting young nun.

CHAPTER SIX

As soon as he judged they were out of hearing, de Soutenay edged his mount towards John. "My liege, I went to great pains to obscure your identity, but what is the point if you will not do likewise?"

John laughed; Giles de Soutenay gritted his teeth.

"My dear de Soutenay, you did not fool those old crones in the slightest. They *knew*. Yes, they knew, and they perceived that I knew. I thought to take example from Brother Richard for once and charm them." He smirked. "I warrant I succeeded full well, especially with the infirmaress. 'Goodwife Nurse' indeed! Did you see the adoration in those old eyes?" He chuckled at the memory. "Nay, Giles, they won't betray me. And the others? Clucking hens who know nothing. They won't betray me, in truth." He nodded, certain of their loyalty. "And it pleases me to know they will be praying for my soul. Heaven knows I need prayer, wouldn't you say? What with my grievous sins, and with my enemies only too glad of a chance to make an end to me and bring that whelp Arthur over. Even Brother Richard prefers him as his heir, rather than troublesome John." The lightness went from his face and his eyes hardened to granite chips. "But the other? The wood nymph? I want her." He leant forward over his mount and lowered his voice, and the menace in his tone chilled Giles' blood. "And the device she used? I want *that*. And I expect you to find them. If I don't miss my mark, she is still in that abbey somewhere." He straightened up, the menace gone from his voice but his eyes still hard. "Yes, I daresay I value that as much as you value your lands, de Soutenay, so I suggest you get back to the Abbey and wait."

Giles started. John was not in a position to take his lands. John saw it and laughed harshly.

"Ah yes, you're thinking it isn't within my power to divest you of your lands. And you are right. It isn't – yet! But it will be. That, upon my soul, I do swear to you." He gave another glittering smile to the fulminating de Soutenay. "As for me?" He turned to his men, laughing once more, "I have a wood nymph to chase, and where better to start than yonder village. Come, let us find some nymphs. I hear they can be most obliging." And with a yell, he kicked his mount into a gallop and went headlong towards the village, followed by his men, whooping and laughing.

Giles watched him leave, a grim expression on his face. A pity he'd thought of taking him to the damned Abbey. But then, had he died, the chaos that would ensue didn't bear thinking of. Richard, as yet, had no heirs, and if rumours were true, it looked as though he might never procreate. He was so busy crusading, his unfortunate bride would, in all likelihood, see little of him. John would make a poor king, but anything would be better than his dead brother's child. For certes, the King of France along with Constance and her ilk would hold the leading reins there. It might lead to civil war again. He shuddered. Tales were still told of the cost of the conflict between Stephen and Matilda. No, he had done the only thing he could and saved John's miserable skin. And was John grateful? Not he! But now they must be sure his enemies didn't discover his fatal reaction to bee stings.

Bee stings! Whoever would have thought it? Without that device, the problems of keeping John safe increased ten thousandfold. *Would that someone else had been with him when it happened. Anyone but me.* And now his lands would be forfeit, for John was right – he would be king, de Soutenay had no doubt of that. He *must* find that device. *And* the woman. Now John had taken it into his head that she looked like a wood nymph, nothing would do but for him to see her. Knowing his lord's insatiable appetite for women, Giles just hoped this one would be willing to satisfy it.

He turned his mount and made to the cover of some nearby trees. Dismounting, he tethered the horse to one of them, then sat hidden beneath the canopy of the largest tree he could find and prepared for a long and boring wait.

A short way from where he was sitting, Etheldreda was coming ever nearer to the Abbey.

CHAPTER SEVEN

The heat of the day and the warmth of the sun were penetrating even the heavy cover of leaf and branch where Giles had chosen to secrete himself from the trail which meandered alongside the woods to the Abbey. It was not the best of paths to take, but better than the track which ran through the deepest part of the woods. He also had a remarkably clear view of the Abbey from this secluded position. The haze of the day was beginning to make him feel drowsy. He needed to change position. Yawning, he got to his feet, stretching until his muscles cracked. Ah, that felt good. He rolled his neck and stretched his arms again. Then, he swatted irritably at the midges which were clustering above him, only clearing them temporarily, and wiped sweat from his brow with the back of his hand, wishing he was within reach of the stream which burbled so merrily in the distance. A large horse fly was hovering threateningly, but he dealt with that, waiting until it landed on Troubadour and swatting it before it could draw blood.

"Poor old boy, what wouldn't you give for a drink from that stream, eh?" The sorrel nosed at his tunic hopefully. "You're in luck, Troubadour, but you knew that, didn't you? You old fraud." Pulling out two apples, he proffered one to the horse, who took it from his open palm and crunched. Giles eyed his own apple thoughtfully, rubbed it on his tunic and took a satisfying bite. "It isn't much, but better than nothing, eh, old fellow?" An unsentimental man, who could be brutish when necessary – and as one of John's men, it was necessary far more often than he would have wished – he lavished what little affection he possessed on this horse of his.

Troubadour, although handsome enough, had nothing more to draw the eye than any other of his horses but responded to his every nuance so well that sometimes it was as if man and horse communed in spirit. There was no time or occasion in Giles' life for any other tender emotions. He had lands, but not extensive ones, and the best he could hope for was for John to accede to the throne and bestow an heiress on him, hopefully a young and beautiful one. There was every possibility of the first. Richard was a warmonger, never happier than when fighting in yet another crusade. The likelihood of his surviving long was remote. It would only take a moment's carelessness. And there would be many plots against his life. It was common knowledge that the French King and the German Emperor hated his guts, and were, in all probability, conspiring against him. And Richard was an absent king; at least, John would likely spend more time in the country he hoped to rule. Whether that would be beneficial to the country or not would remain to be seen. There were those who thought the infant Arthur would be a better choice. *Better the devil you know,* thought Giles. He sat with his back against a tree, eating his apple and waiting to see what his vigil would uncover.

Suddenly, he stiffened. A low-pitched voice came to his ears. Squinting through the leaves which hid him, he could see a figure – a nun, by the look of it. He would be able to see more clearly as she came nearer. But that was no church chant she was humming. He flattened himself against his tree and watched and waited for her to come into view.

Etheldreda had quite overcome her fears by this time. So close to the Abbey and once again in her habit, she felt secure enough to relish the novelty of being out in the fresh air completely alone. She had been enjoying the feel of the sunshine on her face and a rare sense of freedom and had forgotten herself enough to be humming a lay she had remembered from her previous life. She couldn't remember the words – something about a maiden and larks singing.

Her hidden watcher grinned. It was the nun who had dared to cheek him earlier. She would be doing penance for that if anyone heard her. She probably had no idea what the words meant. It was a clever little song which sounded entirely innocent, but it was loaded with double meaning. Ah well, to the innocent all was innocent. And he had no doubt that her soul was as pure as the driven snow, at least compared to his. He sobered as he remembered how many mortal sins he had committed. It was high time he spoke to his confessor. A man could never be sure of living beyond the moment.

Giles shook his head irritably. Enough of this foolishness. He was here to do a job, the development of a spiritual conscience was a luxury he could not afford.

He watched as she strode along. She had forgotten to glide as the nuns usually did, stepping out confidently as she passed his hiding place, her hands not tucked into the sleeves of her habit but swinging in time with her stride. He didn't keep an unbroken stare upon her; if you did that, people oft-times sensed your eyes upon them. Better by far to look away frequently.

As she passed, he noticed something strange. She carried a basket of herbs, but there was something showing from beneath them, poking out from the basket. Giles stroked his chin thoughtfully. *Now just what have you got hidden in there, my fine lady?* Something was afoot. He watched more closely as she continued on her path, eyeing her with renewed interest as she entered the confines of the Abbey.

The nun disappeared behind the Abbey walls, the gates closed, and the Abbey basked peacefully in the afternoon sun. Bees droned, sucking on the small woodland flowers; birds sang and called as they flitted from tree to tree. Had he been aware of his surroundings, Giles could have seen men toiling in the fields, shouting to each other; ploughmen encouraging the oxen, calling as they worked. The heat of the day hung heavily about him but the soft fragrances of the woodlands in which he sheltered were wasted on him; he had but a single focus – the Abbey. He watched and waited patiently, something he was particularly good at. As a child, Giles had been able to stay so still that the adults in his life had often been unaware of his presence, and thus he learnt things which most children would have missed. His sister, Petronilla, used to call him Catspaw, for she swore he moved as quietly as did the sly creature that inhabited the stables and barns. He leaned back against his tree, stretched his legs and dropped his chin onto his chest. Had anyone passed him, they would have thought he was in a deep sleep, except for the fact that his eyelids were not so much closed as narrowed. There was naught he could do now save continue to watch the Abbey.

Etheldreda ceased her humming as she approached the Abbey confines. She had forgotten herself for a few minutes but now slipped back into her more familiar role.

In her chamber, Hildegarde was pacing the floor. Where was Sister Etheldreda? She had been gone for longer than expected. Hildegarde berated herself for sending the nun and prayed she hadn't endangered her. It was her job to protect her flock, not send them out into perilous situations.

CHAPTER EIGHT

I sat there alone in that dark, stuffy cell for what seemed like hours. Why was I in peril? I had no idea what was happening. I had barely got my head around the fact that I had somehow been pulled into another time. With Hildegarde, everything seemed so matter of fact, but here in the silence and the dark, my brain struggled to believe I was not dreaming. I touched the rough straw pallet beneath me. If it was a dream, the sensations seemed remarkably real.

I tried to ignore the panic which was swelling up inside me, clutching at my heart and throat, threatening to rise up out of my mouth in an ear-splitting scream of terror. A cold sweat beaded my forehead, and gooseflesh came up on the skin of my arms. I was deathly afraid that I would be left in here, forgotten in the darkness and even more deathly afraid that I would be found by the men who were seeking me.

A scuffle in the straw confirmed another horror. Mice – or worse! I leapt up, biting my lip to stop myself crying out, then sat back down on my pallet, lifting my feet and curling them beneath me to get them off the floor. But mice could climb, couldn't they? This nightmare was getting worse and worse, and the urge to scream and cry was becoming harder to quell. Deep breaths, that was it. And counting; I counted at the dentist when I had a filling. It helped me stay calm. Maybe it would do the same here. *One, two, three...*

I had counted to fifty when I heard movement, a grunt and a scraping sound. Someone was moving the cupboard which concealed the entry to my hiding place. I froze, wishing I could see something to hide under or behind. Holding out my little lantern, I considered crouching behind the pallet, but it was too low to hide me. Anyway, it was too late. There came the noise of grating, as a key turned in the lock.

Light flooded into my prison. Blinded, I couldn't see for a few moments and squeaked in alarm as a hand grasped mine. Then, the tension left my body as I made out Hildegarde's face bending over me in concern. She pulled me gently to my feet and led me from the cell.

"You poor child. I wish I hadn't had to leave you there in the dark for so long. Come, drink this."

She handed me a goblet filled with what looked and smelled like red wine. I sipped at it gingerly, surprised by the sudden richness that flooded my mouth and sent a comforting warmth through my veins.

"Are you surprised that nuns drink wine?"

I nodded. "I am rather. I thought nuns lived on bread and water."

She laughed merrily. "As did I. It turns out, though, that we eat and drink rather well. We don't have meat often, but our diet is wholesome, and I have an excellent cellarer. Also as Abbess I have, on occasion, to entertain the nobility, so I have some rather fine wines at my disposal. Of course, you may have ale if you wish, but..."

"Wine is fine by me, and this really is good. But I don't understand. Why am I in so much danger? What did I do?"

"It isn't so much what you did, although that comes into it. It's more what you may now be perceived as *knowing*."

"But I don't know *anything*," I wailed.

"Ah, but they think you might. Let me explain."

I wished she would. The fact that I might be in danger frightened me nearly as much as the thought that I might be stuck here forever.

"Marion, the young man who was stung by a bee is none other than John of Mortain – you would know him as Prince John."

She looked at me, obviously expecting me to be impressed. I gazed back blankly. She was out of luck – the name meant nothing to me. I wished, not for the first time, I'd paid more attention at school.

"Marion! What do they teach in schools these days? Very well, let us go through the basics."

Obviously, in whatever time I was, I would be considered an ignoramus.

"Now, the ruler at the moment is King Richard."

"Is he the one who killed those poor little boys?"

"That's the wrong Richard. This is Richard the Lionheart, as you know him. Now, pay attention. Richard has only just married so has no heirs of his own yet, and as he travels extensively and is fighting wars much of the time, to say nothing of plots against him, his lifestyle is not conducive to longevity. John is his brother and potentially his heir. At the moment, Richard has named his other brother's son, Arthur, as heir, but he is a mere babe and is living in France. Richard will probably change his mind. Besides, Queen Eleanor, his mother, would never permit it. Not only does she favour John as heir, but she knows Arthur would be the pawn of the French King, and *that* she would never allow.

"It would suit some if Arthur were to inherit the throne, but it would be disastrous for England and would probably result in civil war. Now if, as it seems, John has developed an allergy to bee stings, and if his enemies were to hear of it, that would make him vulnerable. Do you understand?" She was observing my reactions closely. "I had to play dumb to his men otherwise the convent and the sisters might also be endangered, but I fear John was not deceived. And when he made that clear, I hope I made him believe in my love and loyalty."

The light was beginning to dawn. "And I suppose he wants to make sure I keep my mouth shut?"

Frowning, she fiddled with the large cross she wore. "I'm afraid it's rather more than that. John knows he is vulnerable, and he knows you have a device which saved his life. I think he was more conscious than we realised when you used it."

Comprehension was becoming clearer and clearer. My blood ran cold again, the wine not proof enough against each new, fearful discovery. "But…but it isn't any *use* to him," I stuttered. "It can only be used once."

She looked worried. "Marion, the man is medieval. And he's a lord. He is used to being lied to, and he is used to getting his own way. If it can't be used again, he will want more. If he gets his hands on you, he will want answers. Do *you* want to explain it to him? They have been known to use torture in this age, and John is *not* a reasonable man." She paused, looking at me intently. "You are in 1191 now, Marion."

1191? I blenched, feeling as though my blood was draining out from me.

Hildegarde looked at me, seemingly undecided about something.

I couldn't meet her gaze – I was appalled. This was beyond any nightmare; I've never been so frightened in my life. I grasped the stem of my goblet as though it was a lifeline, raising it to my lips. I am not much of a drinker, but if ever I needed alcohol, it was now. My hands were shaking so much that I needed both of them to hold it steady, and my teeth were chattering so badly, I was afraid I might take a bite out of the goblet. I took a long drink and felt the liquid warm me as it went down. It helped – a little. At least, it eased the shaking. I drained it and set it back on the table.

Hildegarde sat silently watching me, then nodded decisively. "I suppose you'd better know the rest."

There was more? How much worse could it get?

"John is capable of charm and even great kindness, but he is a hard man at heart and petulant. He also has an insatiable appetite for women, and he loves novelty."

I felt the bile rise up in my throat as the implications of this sank in. I had thought I couldn't be any more scared. I wanted to run, but there was nowhere to go. I put my head into my trembling hands and sobbed.

Hildegarde got up and put her arm around my shoulders. "Now, don't despair, my dear. All is not lost. As soon as I realised the danger, I sent Etheldreda to draw them off; she should be back soon. I am hopeful we may have convinced them you left some time ago, but I'm not sure. John is deeply suspicious, by all accounts. There is a strong probability he may have left someone on watch. I don't believe you to be in immediate danger, although we must take care. Right now, my main concern is how to get you back to that tree. We *must* get you back to your own time." She paced the floor, a worried frown creasing her forehead.

I sniffed and scrubbed at my eyes, then suddenly became aware that beneath the almost permanent terror I was in, I was feeling uncomfortable for a different reason and looked around me cautiously. Hildegarde noticed. She was very perceptive, this woman; I imagine she was a very effective abbess.

"Is there a problem, Marion? Apart from the obvious one, I mean? "

I wriggled, not quite knowing how to ask this very prosaic question. "Actually, yes. Um, what do nuns do for bathrooms in this age?" She looked at me and her brow cleared in sudden comprehension. She laughed gently; I wondered why. Surely, we all had the same needs.

"Well, we have very different facilities from the ones to which you are used." She grinned mischievously. "Marion, dear, we have communal lavatories."

I was puzzled. What was the joke? "We have those too."

At this she seemed to be struggling to contain her mirth, not actually laughing, but biting her lip and mopping her eyes with a scrap of fabric. "You do indeed, but not as communal as ours. We have one long bench, with holes but no partitions." I gave her an outraged look, and she finally gave in to the amusement afflicting her, spluttering. "Oh Marion, if you could only see your face."

As I sat there in mortification, she took pity on my shocked condition. "Don't worry, my dear. As Abbess, I have more privileges than wine alone." She moved to part of the wall which was heavily hung with tapestries and raising one hand, she drew aside one of the hangings, opened a door and pointed inside. "My very own garderobe. It is not what you are used to, but at least it gives you privacy." I cannot tell you how relieved I felt as I stepped inside.

When I emerged, Hildegarde had stopped smiling and was pacing the floor again, a worried frown on her face. I gave her a questioning look as I seated myself.

"I'm worried. Sister Etheldreda has been gone longer than I expected. I have prayed for her care but, I confess, I am concerned for her safety." As she spoke, there came a tap at the door, and Etheldreda entered, followed by Sister Ursel.

Relief flooded Hildegarde's face as she ceased her pacing, holding her hands out in welcome. "My child! Oh, *what* a relief. Did it go well?"

Before Etheldreda could answer her, the redoubtable Ursel broke in. "Well enough, if you count the fact that she was nearly taken by one of the men from the village and aroused no end of curiosity as she fled from his advances. It seems she will be remembered by enough, should they be asked. Not to mention being well-nigh gored to death by a wild boar! Thank the good Lord she is back in one piece."

"Thank Him, indeed." Hildegarde ushered the blushing Etheldreda, who seemed not one whit the worse for her adventures, to a chair and poured her a goblet of wine.

Etheldreda, who was hugely enjoying this deviation from her regular routine, sipped at the wine appreciatively. This was not what they were usually given in the refectory. She let the rich taste roll over her tongue and savoured the depth of flavour, the heady aroma of it. Sitting back in the chair as the other two nuns fussed about her, she let the events of the day run through her mind again. It had been terrifying at the time, but she had to admit to a thrill as she relived it all. She still had little idea what was really happening, but she intended to enjoy it. There would be time aplenty to come back down to earth, and it wasn't often such adventure came her way – probably never again. She let the others speak as she relished the wine and tried to glean an understanding of the situation.

Hildegarde turned to me, clasping my ice-cold hands. The heat had penetrated even to within the stone walls of the Abbey, but I was chilled with fear.

"We need to go stealthily, Marion. John may have left watchers."

"We? You're coming back with me?"

"Not back to your time. This is my time now, the time I am meant to be in. But you cannot go to the beech alone, and I cannot endanger my nuns further. I shall bear you company. From now until I have you safely home, you are in my keeping." She took my dress from the basket Etheldreda had handed back to her and shook it out, looking at it doubtfully. "I'm afraid it is sadly creased. We have no time to smooth it."

I smiled despite my tension. "Abbess, it is fashionably crushed. Many fabrics are worn like that in my time. I usually iron it, as I prefer it smooth, but it's actually supposed to be worn like that."

Two astonished pairs of eyes regarded me. The Abbess merely smiled reflectively. Sister Ursel gave a sniff of disgust. "You mean they wear their clothes like this?" She grabbed my dress from Hildegarde and gave it a disparaging look. "Your time sounds right slovenly to me." Receiving a withering look from her tall Abbess, she cleared her throat. "I mean no offence, Marion, dear. My tongue runs away with me sometimes."

"No offence taken, Sister Ursel. I wonder at it sometimes myself, but it does relieve us of one problem at least."

Abbess Hildegarde took the dress from her and gave it back to me. "Wear it beneath your habit, and when we come near to the beech, we can merely remove the outer clothing."

I stripped, self-conscious before Etheldreda's startled gaze at what lay beneath my habit, and stepped into it, putting the voluminous garment back on top.

"Now," Hildegarde said, "we need to make you look a little more like a nun. Tuck your hands into the opposite sleeves, like so." She demonstrated, her hands disappearing into her sleeves.

"Like this?"

"Yes. Good. Now cast your eyes downward and walk demurely; don't stride."

I took a few steps about the room. She smiled. "We'll make a nun of you yet. Hmm, yes, the casual eye will be well enough deceived. If we should meet anyone, keep your eyes down and do not speak."

I nodded in what I hoped was a suitably demure fashion. "And my bag? How shall I carry that?"

"I shall place it in my basket and cover it, so." She laid a piece of cloth over it. "When we reach the tree, you may take the basket through with you. Now we must hurry, 'ere I'm missed." She looked at Ursel and Etheldreda. "As must you, Sisters. We have been closeted here long enough."

They rose, and Ursel kissed me on both cheeks. Etheldreda suddenly gave me a quick hug. "I can scarce believe all this. Truly, I did not expect such happenings when I entered the cloister. I feel as though I am in some dream."

"So do I." I grinned wryly.

"We will pray for your safe return. Come Sister, we must go back to our duties." Ursel plucked at the younger nun's sleeve urgently, and they left the chamber, the confused-looking Etheldreda giving me one last stare as they went. She had not heard nearly enough to understand.

Hildegarde looked thoughtful. "I shall have to explain some of this to her – but later. There is no time now. Wait here."

I watched as she followed them outside, peering around her cautiously. Then, she beckoned me to follow. I gave the room one last look, trying to burn it into my memory – it isn't everyone who gets to see the inside of a medieval abbess's private rooms – and assumed my demure, nun-like posture, hoping Hildegarde was correct in thinking it would deceive the casual eye. I wanted to look about me frantically checking we were not observed, but the wimple made it difficult. If this was how it felt to be a spy, I didn't think I would be very good at it.

Hildegarde glided swiftly in front of me. I tried to glide too, but the skirt of my dress below the already cumbersome habit kept winding itself around my knees, threatening to trip me, making my gait awkward and clumsy. I was desperate to look around me to make sure no one was watching, but didn't dare, keeping my eyes on the hem of Hildegarde's habit instead. But I couldn't keep up with her; I was dropping behind. Fresh panic hit me. The further behind her I got, the more likely someone else would notice me. How to attract her attention? I coughed gently. Starting, she looked around, realising how far behind her I was. She paused, waiting until I caught up. "It's my dress, Abbess. I can't walk very well in it like this."

"I'm sorry, my dear, I should have realised. No matter. Is this pace easier to keep up with?" She slowed. I nodded thankfully and tried to surreptitiously ease my dress from around my knees.

We skirted the grounds, keeping close to the walls. I tried to stop thinking and feeling and just *be* a nun, gliding as best I could. Nothing in my head, blankness on my face, hands clasping each other gently inside my sleeves. Hildegarde just emanated quiet solitude and peace. I must try to do likewise. It wasn't easy.

"You're doing well, Marion. Almost there. See, here is the gate. Now, the porteress will be on duty. I shall just nod at her as we leave; there is no need for you to say anything."

I could feel the curious eyes of the porteress burning a hole in my back, but I guessed she was too disciplined to question her Abbess. I breathed a sigh of relief as we left the Abbey behind us. Hildegarde heard me and turned. "Yes, I feel much the same, Marion, but it isn't over yet. Keep up the deception just a little longer, dear. No more gusty sighs, please."

"Don't nuns ever sigh, Abbess?"

"Not if they don't wish to draw attention to themselves," she responded crisply.

A dishevelled figure was approaching us. I tensed.

"Don't be afraid," Hildegarde murmured, "he will not bother you."

As the figure neared us, it made to skirt around us, bringing out a clapper and shaking it, shouting something I couldn't quite make out in doleful, resigned tones.

"Poor wretch." The tall figure beside me crossed herself and pulled out a rosary. "Another sad creature for our lazar house monks to care for."

I stiffened involuntarily. "Lazar...you mean leper?" Would this nightmare never end?

My voice must have betrayed my feelings, for Hildegarde gave me a searching look.

"And would you have us withhold God's grace from this poor soul, whom man has cast out?" There was reproval in the voice, although she said it kindly enough, and I felt abashed. "Marion, if not for the lazar houses, these poor creatures would be flung out to die. We cannot heal them, but we can provide comfort, food and shelter for their last sorry days. This is a cruel age, and we are God's buffer against the cold."

I said nothing – what was there to say? – and we continued walking in silence. Hildegarde finished her prayers and put away the beads.

Now, there was an expanse of grassy meadow to cross, before we reached the cover of the woods. The old beech tree was in direct view – it still startled me that it seemed smaller here than in my time; I suppose it was many centuries younger – but if we went the straight way, there would be nowhere for me to remove the habit. My heart was pounding, and any minute I expected to hear a shout of discovery behind us. There were people moving about working in nearby fields, and I felt as though every eye was upon me.

It felt as though it had taken forever, but finally, we reached the woods. As we slipped into the blessed cover, Hildegarde paused. "Now, I think we may relax. Take a few moments, Marion. If you feel as I do, then you need a minute or two to recover yourself. I confess, I fear my heart may stop beating."

I looked at her in amazement. She seemed so calm, but when I looked closely, sure enough, there was a tic beating in her eyelid and a pulse throbbing at the side of her head.

"Well done. Now, keep your nerve. We've done the difficult part. All that remains is to reach that tree."

All? Oh, that would be a doddle then.

Hildegarde, apart from that treacherous involuntary twitch of her eyelid, still looked as calm as though she did this every day. As for me, I was hyperventilating. Terrified we would be stopped, terrified I wouldn't be able to break back into my own time, afraid that I might even end up at another point in history. How did I know this would work? How did she? By her own admission, she had never gone back. She seemed calmly assured that it would be easy enough, but she didn't *know*. No one did. We paused for a few moments, and I tried to relax, leaning against the trunk of a tree as though it might lend me its strength.

"Now," Hildegarde said, "shall we resume our journey? Come." She gestured me to move on.

It seemed like an age, as we moved through the woods, but finally, Hildegarde put her hand on my arm to still me and pointed. There, a short way off, in front of my relieved eyes, was the beech. Our circuitous route had taken a while, but now it was ahead of me. It stood, as it would continue to stand for centuries, alone.

Now, there was clear ground between us and it. I wanted to pick up my skirts and run like the wind, but Hildegarde grasped my arm more firmly. I looked at her, not daring to speak. She had her head on one side, listening. She held up her hand. I listened, but heard nothing except for the breeze rustling the leaves. I opened my mouth to speak, but she frowned and held her finger to her lips, and we stood there silently. Shutting my eyes to concentrate more clearly, I realised what was wrong. It was too quiet. A blackbird shrilled its wild alarm and, ever so faintly on the breeze, there came the slightest sound. A snort, like that of a horse. My whole body froze. Hildegarde moved closer and put her mouth to my ear, speaking so softly I could barely make out her voice.

CHAPTER NINE

Giles de Soutenay stirred. An hour or so had passed since the nun had disappeared into the Abbey. He felt once more inside his tunic and pulled out his last two apples. Regarding them with reluctance – they were somewhat shrivelled – he shined one on his tunic and took a bite. The sharp juice teased his tongue, and he crunched with pleasure. He looked at the other, tempted to eat that too, but then remembered his horse. Poor creature, no doubt he would be glad enough of another apple.

Giles raised himself cautiously from where he sat, each step measured and silent, and moved towards Troubadour, who eyed him hopefully. "Shush, boy. Did you think I'd forgotten you?" He fondled the pricked ears as the horse sought out the apple. "Well yes, I had almost, but here, we'll share what I have, eh?" Troubadour whickered softly, and Giles forbore to tease him, holding out the fruit on his flat palm. The large tongue curled around it and swept it up, leaving a little drool behind. Giles wiped his hand on the reddish mane. "I think I'd better untether you; I may need you yet. Now, stay you here unless I call you." The horse turned its liquid eye on him. Mayhap it was a ridiculous thing to speak to his beast as though it understood him, but this horse seemed to have an extra intelligence, and Giles couldn't resist. He had few confidants, and this big beast was the repository of many secrets. Loosening the reins so they were just lightly draped around the tree and would fall if the horse moved, he stood there, hand on its shoulder, watching the expanse that stretched between him and the Abbey.

At last, his wait was rewarded. The porteress opened the gate, and two figures left the Abbey. "Well, well! So our Abbess feels the need to take the air at this hour, does she? Now, that's passing strange. And she takes a companion. A novice by the look of that robe. Well now, I think it is worth taking a much closer look, eh Troubadour? Hush now, don't you give me away."

The nuns were heading towards the cover of the trees a little to his right. From over the way, he saw another figure approaching the Abbey and watched as it picked its way across the ground. A dishevelled figure this, which, as it got closer, Giles noticed, to his horror, was holding a wooden clapper. The clamour echoed through the trees. Shouts of "Unclean, unclean," hung mournfully in the air. Giles recoiled. A leper. Crossing himself, he pressed further into the shelter of the trees and watched as the shambling creature skirted the nuns widely. He saw the taller of the two, the Abbess, cross herself and pull out her rosary. And all the time, the two figures were coming closer and closer.

As he watched, they moved into the shelter of the woods, still to his right. He strained his ears to hear what they were saying. He could hear soft murmurs, but the words were not clear. They were almost out of his sight now, and he would have to move closer if he didn't want to lose them. The trees, which had hidden him so well, were now hiding the two nuns also.

He trod cautiously, noiselessly, through the woods. The voices grew a little louder. A few more feet and he would be able to hear them, even if he couldn't see them. He edged closer. As he did so, he heard a faint snort from Troubadour and froze. Had they heard? He thought not. Just a few more steps, when suddenly, he stepped on a dry twig. The sharp crack that broke the silence sounded as loud as a thunderclap to him. Again, he froze. This time he was sure they had heard him. Their whispers took on an urgency, and suddenly, a figure broke through the trees, running faster than he had expected. Not in a habit now, wearing a garment in some kind of green fabric, which looked strange to his eyes, he could see why she had been likened to a wood nymph.

Crashing through the trees, he broke cover and pounded after her. The Abbess was shouting behind him; he would deal with her later. A pity he had not kept Troubadour by, but there! He was more than a match for this woman, no matter how fleet of foot she seemed.

A pulse thudded in his temple, and he was beginning to gasp, but he was nearing. A few more yards and he would have her. There was nowhere else for her to run.

She fled blindly on, and it seemed to Giles that she must be out of her senses, for she was running directly into the path of a large beech. She was going so fast, it seemed likely she would run full tilt into it. Giles strained harder and closed on her, trying to swerve to avoid rendering himself senseless by crashing into the tree. As he put out his hand to grasp her, she reached the tree. A loud buzzing was in his ears, and he shook his head briefly to clear it, before watching with horrified eyes as woman and tree started to merge. What witchcraft was this? He could not lose her. He *must* not.

CHAPTER TEN

My heart nearly stopped as Hildegarde spoke. "Someone is over there. We must hurry. Remove your habit, then run as fast as you can to the tree. Don't stop for anything, whatever you hear. Run as though your life depends on it, for it very well may."

I needed no second telling. My nerves, already shredded, were in tatters. I fumbled at the habit, trying to get it off me. The Abbess tutted, then took hold of it and dragged it over my head. Momentarily smothered by its dark folds, I could only stand there helplessly, waiting for her to disentangle me. As the habit finally released me from its imprisonment, I gave a small yelp, as her hands caught and tugged a lock of my hair.

"Sorry, Marion, no time for gentleness." She threw the scarf around my head and shoulders. My legs felt like jelly, but I heard the sharp crack of a twig not far behind me, and it galvanised me into action. I gave her a quick kiss. Hildegarde hugged me and whispered, "Go, now. Quickly."

I turned and ran with all the strength I possessed across the open ground, basket bumping against my thigh as I fled.

There was a shout behind me, and I heard feet thundering after me. The Abbess's clear tones cut through the air. "Run, Marion, *run!*" It gave me an extra spurt. My heart was pounding as my feet sped on and on. The beech got closer and closer, and the bees started to buzz in my head again. Gasping for breath, I stumbled against the tree. Again, I felt the pull from it. This time, I welcomed it.

I felt it pulling me into its trunk. My surroundings began to shimmer and fade and then swim back into focus. I could see the ruins and the car park through the black spots in front of my eyes. Leaning desperately towards them, I strained to reach my own time, but a hand seized me from behind, and I was pulled roughly backwards. The car park and ruins disappeared abruptly, and I was flung onto the ground. Winded and terrified, my breath coming in short, ragged gasps, my lungs burning as they fought for air, I could only gaze in horror at the face staring into mine.

He stood over me, tall and muscular, his hand resting on the hilt of the sword he wore at his side. But his was the face of a man who had seen an apparition. If my own face was pale with fear, his was the colour of putty.

From the corner of my eye, I could see Hildegarde running urgently towards us, her veil streaming out behind her.

My captor opened his mouth to speak, but no words came out. He shut it again, looking from me to the beech tree in disbelief. I lay on the ground at his feet, too afraid to move. Crossing himself fervently, he opened his mouth once more and whispered hoarsely, "What witchcraft is this? What are you?"

I couldn't speak; I didn't know what to say. His sword hissed as he pulled it from the scabbard in one fluid motion, bringing it to rest two inches from my heart.

"I don't know whether to flee or to run you through, so I ask you again, *what* are you?"

Suddenly, he became aware of Hildegarde panting up behind him, for he whirled around to face her.

She stood before him, chest heaving, bright spots of colour on her cheeks, but tall and unafraid, as though daring him to spit her on his weapon.

"You! You know about this? What is she?"

"My lord, put aside your weapon; she is no witch."

"So say you? When I saw her start to disappear before my very eyes? Mayhap you are no nun yourself, my lady Abbess, for you seem all too sure of what is happening here. Strange behaviour for a woman of God."

"Well, and if she were a witch, and if I were, how do you intend to stop us? Are you not afraid of her witchcraft? Think you a sword will work against magic?"

His eyes never left her face. She said again, "Put up your sword; it will not help you. Then, I will explain."

"Explain?" He cursed. "How in Hades can you explain this?" He gestured towards me with his sword. "And you, Mistress, move away from that tree, if you please."

I scrambled backwards, away from the tree, my eyes fixed on that unwavering sword point just inches from me. Hildegarde knelt on the ground beside me, flinging one arm protectively around my shoulders, and I could feel the tension in her. Cheeks still flushed, she kept that calm look on her face, fixing her gaze on the wary, unsmiling eyes above us, gesturing him to sit.

"My lord de Soutenay, Marion possesses no magic. Come, sit; for there is a strange tale to be told here. I cannot keep looking up at you, standing there. For pity's sake man, put up your sword and sit, whilst I tell you a story – but do not touch the tree, for I tell you, the magic is not Marion's. It is the tree."

He gawped horror-struck at it and moved away so fast that he caught his foot on a tussock behind him, lost his balance, swore and sat down heavily. Regaining his composure, he leant towards me, taking my arm with a grip of iron. I gritted my teeth and fought against the pain, but I could feel my eyes starting to brim over. I *would not* cry.

Gesturing to Hildegarde with the sword which had never left his other hand, he ordered, "Speak then, my lady Abbess. But you, Madame," he gave me a long, hard look, "are going nowhere. Is that clear?"

The tree had stopped its faint humming now, and the silence around was almost suffocating, as though even the birds and insects did not dare to come closer. The grasp on my arm tightened a little more, the pain worsened, and I could do nothing to stop the tears starting to trickle down my cheeks. De Soutenay gave me a considering look and relaxed his hand very slightly. I scrubbed at my face with my other hand, never daring to take my eyes from his.

"I apologise, Mistress, if you are hurting, but until I know your tale, I regret that I will be retaining my hold on you." I stared back at him, faint with fear, my arm throbbing. He loosened his grip a little more. "See, I have slackened my hold; I do not wish to injure you."

I nodded my thanks, grateful for any softening on his part. He looked at me severely, grey eyes boring into mine like gimlets. "Do not make me regret my leniency, sweeting, or you will come to a new understanding of pain."

"I won't, I promise. And I thank you." What? I was even beginning to speak like these people.

"And now, my lady Abbess, I have acceded to your requests. Speak. Tell me this tale."

Again, the silence yawned between us. Hildegarde frowned slightly. "Where to begin. It is such a long tale and Marion only a very small part of it." She removed her arm from me, sat back on her heels and scrutinised him. "Do you believe in miracles, my lord?"

He nodded. "Holy Church teaches us of many miracles, and so I must believe they are, but, I confess, I have never seen any. Neither do I expect to."

She smiled. "Even when you are looking at one? A strange miracle, I know, but a miracle nonetheless."

CHAPTER ELEVEN

De Soutenay felt at a disadvantage. These two women were unlike any he had ever met before, excepting the Queen herself. And all were agreed, the Queen was a most extraordinary woman.

The terror he had felt on watching the younger one, Marion, disappearing into that accursed tree, had begun to recede, and curiosity was fast becoming his uppermost emotion, but a prickle of unease still ran its icy fingers down his spine. However, he had Marion fast in his grip. She had not disappeared, neither had she cast a spell. In fact, she didn't look much like a witch. His brow lowered. What did a witch look like, anyway? Marion was neither hideously ugly nor alarmingly beautiful. She didn't fit his idea of a demon. And yet…how could a man tell?

On seeing the tears start to run down her cheeks, he had been moved, against his will, to pity and slackened his grip a little. Could he trust her? Still,

if she attempted to escape him, she would pay –
demon, witch, or woman.

The Abbess was regarding him, a slight frown
on her face. He hoped she hadn't seen through the
chink in his armour, the facade of hardness he
wore, but he doubted it; this tall nun seemed to
have an uncanny knack of seeing what lay beneath
the surface. She had a sharp mind, as good as any
man, he decided, and – he almost grinned, but
recalled himself – considerably sharper than some
he knew. He inclined his head. "I'm waiting."

Hildegarde looked at de Soutenay thoughtfully.
She had first thought him to be a very dangerous
man, but it occurred to her, watching his face as he
noticed Marion cry, that this might be a facade.
There might just be a good man under that hard
exterior. If she could tell this aright, it might be
possible to secure his aid.

Lord, guide my words, she prayed silently. Then,
taking a deep breath, weighing each word carefully
before it left her mouth and never taking her eyes
from his face, she began her tale.

"Before I begin, a question. Do you like John?"
She gave de Soutenay a measuring look. He
scowled.

"I..."

"No, indeed! As I thought. And sometimes you
wish him dead?"

He flushed.

"But consider. If anything should happen to Richard, would you *want* Arthur to rule?"

"What? And become a vassal of France?" He bristled with indignation. "I think not! Why these questions? Begin your tale."

Hildegarde had discovered what she needed to know. Now she could begin.

"My lord de Soutenay, believe me when I say that had not Marion been here today, Lord John would have died."

He looked puzzled. "Your infirmaress said there had been a miracle. I thought it was wrought at her hands."

"No indeed. Sister Ursel has no knowledge of how to deal with this. It would appear John's difficulties arose because he was stung by a bee. Is that not so?"

"Aye, that would seem to be the cause. But I've seen nothing like it before. How can a bee cause death?"

"Indeed. It is unusual, but when a sting causes a reaction as severe as this, it is always fatal – in our world, at least. John was dying when you brought him to us. Sister Ursel could have done nothing."

He blenched and looked at me. "Then, she…"

"Yes, Marion had with her a device which is not known here. John saw it, yes? And he wants it?"

"Aye." He jutted his chin in my direction. "And he wants *her*."

Hildegarde's lips tightened grimly. "Yes. He would. Take a close look at her, my lord. Does she seem like the women you are accustomed to? Marion, lower your shawl, if you please."

I questioned her silently, my eyes saying what I could not. She nodded, and I let the shawl slip from my head, shuddering beneath his searching gaze.

"Look at her hair. Do the ladies of your acquaintance wear theirs like this?"

"You know they do not." He fingered my chin-length hair, and I gritted my teeth, resisting the impulse to jerk my head away. "Stay Mistress, I will not harm you. But the ladies I know wear their hair long. And braided most often – although not always..." He trailed off, grinning at some memory. I had no idea what he meant. Hildegarde seemed to understand only too well.

"Yes, I'm sure!" She cut in on his musings with asperity. "Now, take a look at her garment. Have you ever seen the like on women from our time?"

Letting go of my hair, he took hold of my dress, rubbing the fabric thoughtfully between his fingers, then started as though her words had suddenly struck home. *"Our time?"* He let go of my skirt and whirled back round to face her. Hildegarde stared intently back at him.

"My lady Abbess, you jest!"

She held his gaze calmly. "You can see that I do not."

He swallowed; I could see him struggling to speak. Finally, he forced the words out. "Then, what the blazes...I can scarcely believe I am saying this...cannot credit that I believe you. And yet I do." He turned back to me. "What...*time*...are you from?"

Again, I looked to Hildegarde for guidance.

"Tell him, Marion."

"Twenty oh six," I muttered, trying not to make it sound quite so weird. I needn't have bothered.

"WHAT?" he thundered, leaning closer, those hard grey eyes boring into mine. "Surely, I misheard you?" I shook my head and ventured a smile. I was beginning to feel a bit sorry for him. He looked quite ill.

"No, my lord, you heard true." What *was* it with this place? I found, yet again, that I was speaking like them. It seemed to come quite naturally.

"Twenty-hundred-and-six?" he whispered, voice hoarse. It did sound rather worse, put like that. Sweat started to dot his forehead. *"Two thousand-and-six years?"*

"Give or take a few," I murmured.

"No! No! No!" He let go of my arm, leapt to his feet and paced wildly, running his hands through his hair. "How can I believe this...this...fairy tale?"

"How can you not?" Hildegarde asked. "You saw for yourself how she started to disappear into the tree," she continued as serenely as if this happened every day. "The tree is the gateway between her time and yours. I know this for certes. It was my gateway too."

"You?" he exclaimed in thunderstruck tones. She nodded. "You come from her world?"

"Not her time. I come from my own time, the nineteen-seventies."

He stopped his pacing and looked at her speechlessly. I really was starting to pity him. It must be even harder for him to believe than it had been for me. I, at least, had the evidence of my own eyes and time to have become accustomed to the idea.

"I was training to be a doctor – a healer. One day, I stumbled through this tree just as Marion did. They took me to the infirmary, as they did her. Again, there was urgent need of my skills. Skills which those of your time do not possess."

"But…you stayed."

"I stayed. I believed I had found my calling."

"Then, *she* can stay. I regret, Marion, I need to take you to my liege lord."

"No!" Hildegarde was sharp. "She cannot! And you may not take her. She is not free to go with you. She has a husband, children, a family in her own time. *I* did not. I say again, you may not take her."

He bent down and grasped my arm again, hauling me to my feet. I closed my eyes in despair. I could not see how she would win this argument, and my future looked bleak.

"Nevertheless, I shall take her. If not, my lands will be forfeit. What John wants, John gets."

"And would you take a woman of your acquaintance to John? Your sister? Your cousin?"

"Heaven forfend."

Hildegarde's voice was hard. "Then, you will not take Marion."

De Soutenay's face darkened with fury, and my blood chilled. "And who will stop me?"

Hildegarde remained calm. "Your own good sense. Which does John want most? The woman? Or the device she carries?"

His brow furrowed. "The device, I suppose."

"Then, listen to me. That device works only one time. Marion has already used it on John, so now it is worth nothing. Imagine how he will respond when he gets a broken device."

He glared. "Imagine how he will respond when he gets neither device nor woman! If I cannot give him the device, then I swear he shall have the woman."

"I'll tell him it doesn't work," I yelled desperately. "I'll tell him you broke it. I'll tell him you want him to die."

He dropped my arm as though I had suddenly grown fangs. "You bitch," he swore. "He'll not believe you."

"Oh no?" I hissed into his face. "Who does he fancy? So who will he believe? You want to try me?"

Hildegarde's stern tones cut between us. "Marion! My lord! Stop this. It will not help. Think, de Soutenay. What if John is stung again and the device doesn't work?"

He snarled, "Then, he'll die. Do I care? Once dead, he cannot avenge himself on me."

"Yes, he'll die. And who, then, will accede to the throne? Arthur? Think you the French will reward your loyalty to John?"

He strode back and forth like a man demented. I wondered whether I should take the chance. Could I reach the tree before he got me? Measuring the distance, I hesitated…and was lost.

As if he'd read my mind, his hand shot out and seized me again. "Think not to outwit me, Madame. If it came to a struggle, which of us would win, think you?"

I subsided into silence, my arm still firmly in his grip. Tears of frustration started to well up again. I took a deep breath and swallowed hard. He was right. This was a man trained to fight. I had no defence against him. His muscles were iron hard. I didn't even have shoes on my feet, couldn't even kick him with any effect. If I clawed at his face, I would come off worse. I vowed to buy a pepper spray if ever I got home. If only I had one in my bag. It was the one thing which might have deterred him, yet I pitied him almost as much as I feared him. This was an impossible situation.

De Soutenay let go of me again and resumed his pacing. He had pulled at his hair so much it was in complete disarray. "Then, all is lost. I may as well hand over my lands to John right now. Or maybe go direct to France and offer my sword to the French King. For certes, I lose everything I have here."

Hildegarde rose, placing a hand on his shoulder. She was nearly tall enough to be able to look directly into his eyes. "No. All is not lost. Sit you down, and let me think."

He grimaced. "For a woman, you seem very able, my lady. Of a surety, you argue like a lawyer."

She gave me a wry look. "Sadly, Marion, men are even less likely to listen to women in this age. Now, hear what I have to say, but first, what is your given name, my lord de Soutenay? I really cannot keep calling you that."

"Giles."

"Very well, Sir Giles. Now, this may surprise you both, but it is not in Marion's interests either to let the French King rule England."

I looked at her in surprise. "It isn't? Why should I care? I come from the future."

"You certainly do. But your ancestors, my dear, come from the past. What would happen to you if history as you know it – although I'm very much afraid you don't know it at all well – were to change?"

A sudden recollection of all the films involving time travel rushed at me. Marty disappearing from the photo in that film about the DeLorean – I could never remember the name – it had Michael J. Fox in it. Everything I had seen on Doctor Who. If history as we knew it never happened, what would happen to me? And what would happen to my girls? I shook my head. This was getting ridiculous. It was beyond a joke. I could not believe I was sitting here discussing it, and yet…here I was. And this morning, I would have said that was ridiculous too.

"So what is supposed to happen, Abbess? What is our history?"

She looked thoughtfully at us both. "I suppose it can't hurt to tell you. Sir Giles, if you should breathe a word of this…"

"They would think me deranged. Never fear, Abbess, I shall not be telling tales."

"Exactly what I was going to say. And Marion, if your girls were to hear about this, how do you think they would react?"

I gawped at her. She had summed them up without even knowing them. It spoke volumes for her knowledge of human nature. Chloe would get to that tree by hook or by crook, and if, by some unlucky chance, she got through, it didn't bear thinking about.

"And so we three are bound together. We dare not share this with another living soul. Very well, I shall tell you what I remember, although," she said with a grimace, "I must admit it was a very long time ago. Or ahead. Depending on which way you look at it. Now, attend please. Sir Giles, you already believe Richard will not be long lived, as, I'm sure, does John. You are right. In the not too distant future he will die, but before he does, he will have named John as his heir. Yes, Richard will forgive him for his part in certain, um, plots. Eleanor will make sure of that. For, depend upon it, she will not want England ruled by a French king. She has no love for them."

She and Giles shared a sidelong glance. I felt rather left out and resolved to study history when...if...I got home.

"And yes, John will rule. Whether or not you will lose your lands, Sir Giles, I cannot say. I am not as well acquainted with history as that. I'm afraid you have no major part in the history books, for which you should be grateful." She laughed. "It so often seems that people with a large part to play in history meet with untimely deaths. Be glad your fate is largely unknown, mayhap it means you will have a long and happy life. But we can almost say for a surety that, should John be allowed to die, you will lose your lands. The French King will have them off you before you can say, 'I yield.' And, Marion, if John does not rule, who is to say you will find your family still as you left them in your time? And so it behoves us to find a way out of this plight. Be still both of you, and let me think." She walked a little away from us, then knelt, hands clasped before her, head tilted skyward as if in prayer.

I glanced at Giles, a little more at ease after Hildegarde's good sense had struck home for both of us. "It looks as though we'll have to work together."

He smiled back and looked a lot less terrifying. "In truth, I will admit I was not easy in my mind about handing you over to John. The Abbess is in the right of it, I would not want that for any lady of my acquaintance. Oh, he would reward you right well, but it is not a life you would want, I think."

He could say that again. I'm a one man woman, and I love my Tom. I didn't care whether this John was a prince or not. I wanted to go home.

"So tell me. Is it much different to our time, where you are from? And how did you come to be here – apart from that wretched tree, I mean."

"Oh yes." How could I tell this man about cars, planes, computers? I wouldn't know where to start. "Very different. We have ways of communication you couldn't begin to imagine, ways of travel that would blow your mind." Oops! I was reverting to my own century. But how on earth else could I express myself better?

"Blow my mind?" He gave me a bemused look. "Your speech differs too. I can imagine faces here, should I use that expression. Blow my mind." He lingered over the words, a tentative smile spreading across his face again, transforming the stern features into something much more amenable, rather attractive in fact. I confess, I quite liked it.

"Well, I think I'd put it out of my mind, if I were you. I can't imagine it would go unnoticed."

A sudden handclap distracted us. Hildegarde was sitting bolt upright, hands together, her face lit up. "I have it. We shall use the tree. Marion, if not injected immediately, how long do these devices last?"

"It's hard to give you a definite time. I've had some that have barely lasted a year."

"I see. Very well, let me consider."

She sat for a moment, lost in thought, then brightened and turned to me again.

"Then, might I ask you to help Sir Giles keep his lands? And maybe save his life? John can be vengeful, and in helping him, you would help yourself. For if history unfolds as it should in our history books, all will be well with your family too."

Yes, I could see that. Besides, I didn't want to put Giles in danger. I was beginning to see the man beneath. There was more to him under that hard exterior than met the eye. I wished him no ill. If I could help him, I would. Besides, Hildegarde was right. Who knew how my life might be affected? If history changed, what would I return home to find? But how? How could I help him?

Hildegarde read the question in my eyes. "Marion, can you get more of these devices? Say, one a year?"

"Possibly." I couldn't get them on prescription, that was a certainty. I would have to try to get them over the internet. They reckon you can get most medications online; hopefully, it wouldn't be considered illegal. It was pretty common knowledge people got all sorts of stuff that way which could usually only be bought with prescriptions. I could probably do it. I hoped so.

She raised her eyebrows. "Possibly? No guarantees?"

"It would be difficult. Listen, Abbess, you trained to be a doctor. How would you treat someone who kept claiming to have lost their child's medication? Or who kept claiming she had been stung?"

"Hmm, I do see the problem."

"But we do have more access to meds than in your day. I might be able to get them online." The eyebrows went higher. "Too difficult to explain, and I couldn't vouch for their efficacy. Online goods are not always genuine, but it's the best I can do."

"Then, we shall have to be content with that. There is always the possibility John will not be stung again." She grinned mischievously. "Indeed, I do not recall history recording any such incident. It may be that your contribution to the archives will never be told, that the secret will be kept." She looked at me soberly now. "And do you think you would be prepared to approach the tree again? For I know of no other way for you to reach us."

I stiffened. No way did I ever want to go near that tree again – not in my lifetime. She watched my reaction and touched my arm. "Don't be afraid. I would not ask you to put yourself at risk. I may be wrong, but I do not believe it is necessary for you to come though into our time again. Look, see?" She pointed to a hollow half hidden in the roots of the tree. I leaned forward. Giles grabbed my arm again and leaned over me, craning his neck to see what she was pointing at. "When you started to return to your own time, half of you was still visible in our time. Is that not so?" She looked questioningly at Giles.

He grinned at me, white teeth showing against his tanned skin. "I've never seen aught like it. I thought you were a demon. It was only instinct made me reach for you. Had I time to think, I would not have touched you."

"Exactly. Now Giles, you will need to trust me. Let go of Marion, if you please. And Marion, do I have your word that you won't go through that tree until I have finished explaining?" I nodded, rubbing my bruised arm. "Then, give me your hand. Come." She took my hand and drew me closer to the tree. "Bend down here." She knelt, and I followed suit. Tugging at me a little, she moved my hand close to the roots. "Now, I will hold your arm, and you place your hand in this hole here. Let us see what will happen. Hark?" She held her hand up. "Can you hear it?" A faint hum was coming from inside the tree. Fainter than before.

Nervously, I placed my hand where she had suggested. Giles was close behind us, I could feel his breath in the nape of my neck. As my hand went into the hollow, my fingers started to disappear. I pushed in further. Now my hand was missing up to the wrist. It went through my mind that this was my chance to escape, but I knew I daren't. Who knew what I would find on the other side? If it was true that I was here for a purpose, what would happen if that purpose was never accomplished?

Hildegarde pulled me away, and my hand came back into view. I flexed my fingers. Turning, I saw that Giles' face was white again. He bit his lip.

"Now," Hildegarde said as calmly as if I had not started to disappear before her eyes, "it may be that your job has already been done. That in saving John's life this one time, you have secured history. But if not...if he were to be stung again..."

She was right. We couldn't be sure.

"And so what I am suggesting is this. We need to renew the device once a year, is that correct?" She looked at me, and I nodded. "Yes, it is as I understood it then. And so we depend on you being able to get a device every year. It may be that you will be unable to do so. If such is the case then nothing can be done, but..." She held up her hand as Giles opened his mouth to speak. "No, hear me out. So you will do your best, Marion. And once a year, let us say on Whit Monday, you will come to the tree and try to put the device there." She indicated the hole in the base again. "We cannot guarantee this will work, but it is all we have. Are you agreed?" I nodded. My part could be done. "And you, Giles. You will also be here on Whit Monday each year. You will pass back the old device." She laughed, "For we cannot have plastic cluttering up our forests in this day and age. Whatever next!" Giles looked at her, plainly baffled. "Yes, I know you don't understand, but you agree it would be problematic if anyone but you and John saw it, yes? Do you agree to do this?"

"What choice have I? But what of this year? I need to present John with that device now." He turned back to me. "How quickly can you get one? For me, the case is urgent. Your world may be as normal when you go back, but if I can neither produce you nor it, my life is like to be short and unpleasant."

I could understand his point of view. And so grateful was I that I wouldn't be presented to John in place of the epinephrine, I would do my best to help. Besides, I didn't want Giles on my conscience. John sounded like a most unpleasant prince.

I considered. How long might I need? I had to find a source and then get it delivered, but I couldn't be sure how long that would take. "Could you let me have a week to find out? I could put a note through to let you know. Or, wait. Could you tell John that I have to obtain a new device? That this one can't be used again? Tell him you will be able to fetch it at Whitsuntide if you like. Will that sound magical enough for him?" That was about three weeks from now. Surely, I could get one by then.

He looked mutinous. "Mayhap I should go through that tree with you."

I recoiled in horror. I could barely imagine how well he would fit into the 21st century! He'd probably get himself arrested within a week, and how on earth would I explain him to Tom and the girls?

Again, Hildegarde intervened with calm good sense. "Why not wait until Whit Monday? If Marion fails us, then the decision is yours." She gave him a steely look. "However, I would not recommend it. You cannot begin to understand how things will have changed. Likely, you would find yourself in even more serious trouble there. Here, if the worst happens, you can always flee to France."

He stood there, indecision clear on his face, brow furrowed in concentration. I felt sorry for him. The poor man was in a horrible position. Moving to him, I placed my hand on his arm. He looked at me helplessly, lost.

"I will honestly try my best." I tried to sound reassuring. "If it isn't beyond the realms of possibility, I will help you."

He took my hand from his arm and held it between his own large ones as if trying to convey his anxiety to me. The sunlight glinted on a heavy ring set with a garnet, red as wine, on the little finger of his left hand. This time, I felt no fear of him; his touch was almost tender.

"I thank you, Marion. And I am sorry. The Abbess is in the right of it. I'd not want a woman of my family surrendered to John. I see now, I couldn't have done it. But I do most earnestly implore you not to fail me, for if you do, you condemn me to poverty and I know not what else. John is unpredictable and dangerous when thwarted." He leant forward and touched his forehead to my own. "Marion, don't let me down."

Silence hung in the air, and I was almost painfully aware of the bond this stranger-than-fiction experience had forged between us. Not love, well, not on my side anyway, but I suppose you could call it a kind of kinship. Not friendship, something more meaningful. At any rate, we had touched each other's lives and hearts in some way across aeons of time. I moved my head and looked into his eyes; he held my gaze. "I won't. If it can be done, I promise you, I'll do it."

Hildegarde came to us, and the spell that bound us was broken. "Come now. The longer we tarry, the more danger there is of our being discovered."

Her words brought me back to my senses. Giles let go of me but as he did so, Hildegard seemed to look strangely at his hands. Did she disapprove? She didn't seem the disapproving type. She seemed, to me, to have an understanding of human nature I had never encountered before. Maybe it was her faith, maybe just her experience of life. She must have seen more than most.

She hesitated as if lost in thought and put her hand to her neck, pulling a string out from beneath her scapular, fiddling with it, removing something. Then, reaching for my hand, she opened my fingers, placed something which felt like a pebble in my palm and closed my fingers around it. "Don't open your hand yet," she said quietly, as though she didn't wish Giles to hear her, "but take this to remember me by. It doesn't belong here in this time; take it back to its rightful place for me. Wear it sometimes and think of me, dear Marion, for you somehow feel like kin to me."

She kissed me lightly on my forehead and murmured a benediction. Then, "Are you ready?" I nodded.

Giles, who had moved away, suddenly swung back towards me, seized me and kissed me soundly on the lips. I'm ashamed to say, for a moment, I felt myself starting to respond – maybe it was the unexpectedness of it – before he whispered, "Marion, again I ask you, don't fail me. Fare you well, and may God be with you." He stepped back and stood alone a little apart from Hildegarde, his expression sombre.

Hildegarde handed me the basket containing my bag and walked with me to the tree. The buzzing had started again. I began to feel the same pull as last time and leaned towards it, straining to see through the mist which lay before me. Then, I turned back for one last glimpse of Hildegarde and Giles and watched them shimmer and fade before my eyes as I moved out of their world and back into my own.

The buzzing eased; the mist cleared, and the car park started to appear before me. I stepped through the tree and saw the Abbey once again in ruins. I looked behind and saw nothing but the huge trunk of the ancient beech. Giles, Hildegarde, everything from that time was gone. It even felt as though it was fading from my mind. Had it all been a dream?

I stepped away from the tree, caught my foot in my dress and toppled towards the ground. As I put out my hands to break my fall, a small object fell from my fingers. Landing heavily, I lay there winded for a few moments, watching the object roll away from me before reaching out to grasp it. It glimmered brightly in my hand; a gold ring set with a garnet which looked vaguely familiar to me for some reason. As I slid it onto my index finger, I realised it truly had been no dream, no fantasy. It really had happened, and now I was committed to keep a promise for years and years to someone I would never see again. It was a strange, eerie feeling.

As I sat up, the tree vibrated again. I watched as a hand came through the trunk and placed my sandals neatly beside it. The hand hovered for a second, then withdrew. I had wondered what had happened to them. They must have fallen off when I first fell through into the past. Looking ruefully at my dirty feet, I shrugged; there wasn't much I could do about them now.

As I slipped my sandals back on, a shout of, "Mum!" made me look up. Chloe was sprinting across the field towards me, Shannon hard on her heels.

"Did you fall over?"

"Are you okay?"

"We wondered where you were."

"We thought you'd got lost."

"Didn't you have your phone switched on? We rang and rang."

They panted out the words, butting in on each other in their anxiety. I put my arms out to draw them close, so relieved to be back with them. The other place was magical, fascinating, but this was where I belonged, with my family. Now I was finally safe, their hugs melted the last of the fear from my heart, and we turned and walked back towards the ruins, away from the old beech tree.

CHAPTER TWELVE

1191

Giles sat on the grass a few feet from the beech tree, watching as Marion disappeared and resisting a powerful urge to step forward into the mist which surrounded her. He suppressed a shudder; it was unsettling to watch someone fade into nothing before his eyes. The Abbess may have assured him it was not witchcraft, but it still felt dark and dangerous to him. He stilled a superstitious dread that maybe she *had* been a witch after all.

No! No witch, she. I would have known it of a surety when I kissed her, he told himself. *I've kissed enough women to know.* He admitted to feeling a flash of desire for her, but it was no more than that, brought on, he supposed, by the strangeness of the bond they now shared. That, and the fact she was like no other woman he had ever met.

And had she been an enchantress, she would have cast a spell on me then – had me in her thrall. Had she been a witch, I'd have known it then.

So since he was neither spellbound nor out of his wits, why did he now feel so bereft? Hell's teeth! The woman had only been in his life a scant while. He felt no lust when he kissed her, beyond that first sudden urging, had just responded to it, and that response was coupled with the desire to find out for sure whether she be enchantress or no.

Lost in his thoughts, he started when an enquiring nose whiffled at his hair. "Troubadour! What? You are here? Well, and I did not fasten you so tightly after all, in case I had need of you. But there, we'll be on our way soon enough." The big horse nudged him and, getting to his feet, Giles gathered the reins.

For a moment, he'd forgotten the Abbess. She stood there tall and serene, one hand on Troubadour's shoulder. "A nice creature," she said approvingly, then, gazing at him, her greenish-grey eyes assessed him shrewdly. "Unsettling, is it not, watching the tree at work? And doubtless you begin to wonder whether what you have seen be truth. I know the events of the day may seem passing strange…" Giles gave a snort of derision. "Quite so," she continued unruffled. "But be assured of this. She was as real as you or I. Despite what you have seen, hold fast to that truth. Now," she said, turning back towards the Abbey, "you have a difficult task ahead of you. Walk back to the Abbey with me. We have a short while before I must be about my business. Let us discuss a plausible tale – one as near the truth as possible – to tell John. That is, if you wish for my help." She paused, a quizzical expression on her face.

"For a woman of God, my lady, you seem remarkably untroubled by all this and by the planning of falsehoods to be told to my liege lord." He eyed her narrowly as they walked.

"My lord, I am, as you say, a woman of God, so why should I be surprised by the miraculous?" She gave another of her quiet smiles. "And as for falsehoods; there are many ways to tell a truth, are there not? We have merely to decide on the most believable truth for John. I shall leave you to embroider the linen for him. I find, in some cases, men are far better at embroidery than women."

The woman was irrepressible! As Giles could think of nothing to say to this piece of wit, he fell silent.

"It will be time for Vespers soon. Mayhap you would like the use of a guest room? You may wait there and join me for a light supper in my chamber before Compline. We will, of course, be accompanied; I do not entertain in my rooms alone, however, we may speak freely before Sister Ursel. Indeed, she may well be able to assist us. Now, I must think. I urge you to turn your mind to the matter in hand. We have but a short time, and it will be none so easy to come up with something to make John accept your reasons for having neither Marion nor the device."

Giles blenched. A cloud of dread seemed to hover above him; his next meeting with John would be no pleasant one. Distracted, he followed the Abbess, who led him to the chamber where they had previously taken John and took her leave of him.

CHAPTER THIRTEEN

As he rode into the castle bailey, Giles was
immediately accosted by a steward who called a
groom over. John must have had them on the
watch for him. He dismounted and handed over
the reins, patting Troubadour as he was led away.

"My lord de Soutenay." The steward gestured
with some urgency. "Please follow me."

"What? Hellfire, man! Is there no time for a gulp
of wine and to make myself decent?" His hopes for
a chance of refreshment and to wash the grime of
the road from his face and hands thwarted, he
looked ruefully at his sweat-soaked gambeson.
Damn John. Ah well, if he wanted Giles in his dirt,
then that was how he should see him; too bad if the
royal nostrils were offended.

The steward had the grace to look abashed. "I
regret, sire, I was instructed to bring you to Lord
John the moment you arrived."

Striding through the castle behind the steward,
he hesitated at the open door to John's private
chamber and swallowed, wishing there had been at

least time to slake his thirst before the ordeal ahead. Hell's teeth, but his throat was dry.

He'd spent the last night and most of this day going over and over how to explain Marion and the device. Whichever way he ran it in his mind, it had not ended well. Now, still undecided about exactly what to say, the reckoning was at hand; he could put it off no longer. Reluctantly, he followed the steward in, swallowing again. The lump in his throat remained.

John was dicing with some of his men, showing white teeth against his beard as he laughed. Giles saw curious glances in his direction, some sympathetic, others openly hostile. You couldn't be at court long without making enemies, especially if you were thought to be in John's confidence.

John looked up, his brow darkening when he saw Giles' face. Studying him for a second, he caught his full bottom lip between his teeth, then brought his fist down hard on the edge of the table, his eyes narrowed in temper. A child sitting on a chest, almost hidden in the window embrasure, jumped nervously, not quite suppressing a tiny squeak as the table overturned with a crash, sending goblets and flagon tumbling across the floor.

John looked disconcerted for a moment. He had not noticed the child, a daughter of one of his earls, when she had slipped into the room. For certes, she should not have been there, but John was quite fond of children. He crossed to her side in three strides and flung an arm around her thin shoulders. "Nothing for you to be concerned about, sweeting. Run you along, now. I feel sure your mama will be angered with you if she discovers you here."

The child regarded him solemnly, then smiled sweetly and left the room, followed by one of John's favourite hounds.

"I'll warrant she'll be a comely wench when she is older. Well, de Soutenay? I see by your face that you have failed. Do I need to remind you of the penalty?"

"My lord," Giles broke in desperately, "I have not failed, but what I have to say should be in private."

John gave him a considering look and flicked his fingers. "My lords, I regret, I require a private audience with de Soutenay."

Giles looked at the men standing around, some watching intently, others pretending to ignore him. At John's command, they filed out. De Braose glared at Giles, deliberately jostling him as he barged past. Adam Goodwin gave him a hefty clout on the shoulder and an encouraging wink. At least he had a few good friends at court.

John stalked to the table, which had been stood upright again, and poured himself a goblet of wine from a fresh flagon which one of his squires had hastily replaced the old, spilled one with. He looked Giles up and down, reminding him of a cat toying with its prey before the kill.

"You stink!" John took a swallow of the wine, wiped his mouth and gestured to Giles. "I daresay your throat is passing dry. Help yourself."

Relieved – he had thought he would have to croak out his news through a mouth which was still filled with the dust of the road – Giles poured a large measure and tossed it back.

John smiled mirthlessly at him. "Now, I believe you are about to explain yourself." His smile seemed more of a snarl; Giles felt his heart drop to his stomach. "It had better be good." The sentence was said without venom. Indeed, his tone was almost cordial, but it fooled Giles not one whit.

Giles opened his mouth to speak, but before he could utter a word, the door swung open. John turned, a reprimand on his lips. It was never uttered.

A woman stood in the doorway. Tall and straight, her poise belied her years, as her catlike eyes swept around the room. Eleanor of Aquitaine, Queen of England. Most women her age were withered crones, yet Eleanor still retained a trace of that legendary beauty, even though she was in her late sixties; it was no wonder her enemies called her Melusine. Head held high, she picked her way elegantly across the room, her red and gold mantle trailing behind her.

Giles bent his knee before her, and she held out her hand to receive his kiss. "Your servant, my lady."

Her greenish eyes surveyed him coolly. "De Soutenay, I hear you have been on a mission for my son. Pray, rise and seat yourself. John..." She turned to him, holding out her hands.

John took them and dutifully kissed her cheek. "Madame."

"No doubt you wonder why I am here."

John's eyes narrowed. "I feel sure you will tell me in your own time," he said with an edge to his voice, pouring her a goblet of wine. She inclined her head to him, taking a sip of the wine and seating herself in his favourite high-backed chair. John flashed a look of anger, quickly veiled, before seating himself on a lower chair to her left.

"I trust I find you in good health, ma Mère."

"You find me concerned, John. I understand it should be I who am enquiring after your health. Is that not so?" She fixed him with her unblinking gaze.

Fascinated by this exchange, Giles watched as John reddened slightly under her quizzical stare; whether with annoyance or embarrassment he couldn't tell.

"I daresay you intended to tell me about your unscheduled stop at Sparnstow Abbey, my son. I feel sure you were trying to find the appropriate moment to allay my motherly concerns."

John looked warily at her. "How well you know me, Madame. I am, indeed, surprised you have the time to worry over my health. I would have thought there was enough on your trencher."

"Passing strange, John, for I would have said the same of you. However, know that I always will find time to pay attention to my children's welfare." Despite the amused tone of her voice, Giles sensed a veiled warning in the words. And in truth, John had other matters, more urgent than wood nymphs, to attend to.

John fixed her with a slightly hostile stare. "Indeed, ma Mère, it is a pity you were not always so inclined."

He scored a hit; a slight flush flared briefly on Eleanor's cheeks, and her brow puckered almost imperceptibly before she rejoined with, "I feel sure de Soutenay does not wish to be privy to all our family matters. Perhaps this can be discussed at a later date."

Giles lowered his gaze. These Angevins mesmerised him; there was little love evident between them, yet he felt Eleanor did indeed have some maternal affection for John, despite their verbal sparring. Perhaps it was not the love which was missing from their relationship so much as the trust. Little wonder, when John had been implicated in more than one plot against Richard, England's King, Eleanor's favourite. What unloving sons this beautiful woman and her ardent husband had produced as they blazed a trail through England and France. Their love story had set half the world alight yet ended in acrimony and recrimination. It seemed the same warring natures had been inherited by their sons, of whom only two remained – and they at each other's throats.

Richard did seem sometimes to harbour a careless fondness for his younger brother, forgiving him his part in various intrigues, yet punishing him by naming his nephew, Arthur, son of his dead brother Geoffrey, as his heir.

John, on the other hand, Giles was sure, wanted nothing more than to see Richard dead. For the time being, he was playing the part of dutiful brother but fooling no one except, possibly, Richard.

Eleanor put her head on one side, resting her chin on her hand. "Enough of this. De Soutenay, have you procured the device my son desires so much?"

Taken by surprise at the speed with which the conversation had swung to include him, Giles jumped slightly, spilling a drop of wine onto the floor where it lay for a second like a bead of blood before seeping into the rushes.

John gave that peculiarly mirthless smile of his again. "I see my mother's grasp of the situation has startled you, Giles. Myself, I have learned long since that she has spies with an ear to every door, an eye to every crack."

"Spies, John?" The slitted eyes were amused. "I prefer to think of them as safeguards. Certainly, their care is all for you.

"My lord de Soutenay." Eleanor turned her glittering gaze on Giles. "I believe this device I have heard of is needful for my son's continued health. Do, pray, tell me whether or not you have obtained it for him." She drummed her long fingers on the small table set before her.

Giles resisted the urge to fidget like a small boy and returned the cool stare with a confidence he was not feeling. Reaching for his goblet, he took another gulp of the heavy red wine to try to moisten his mouth while he considered how best to reply. Eleanor's fingers continued to beat an impatient tattoo on the wood.

"My lady, I found the woman who had the device."

John leaned forward, his expression avid with lust. "And was she, indeed, a wood nymph? Did she, mayhap, disappear before your very eyes?"

Giles swallowed. That was exactly what had happened, but he could not expect John to believe him.

"Why have you not brought her to me as I demanded? Did she, perchance, bewitch you? And while we are about the subject, Giles," his smile was unpleasant, "was it necessary of you to choose the soubriquet Jankin? Disguise is one thing, but you made me sound like some half-witted churl—"

"John!" Eleanor interjected sharply. "I thought we were agreed on this. Whether or no he brings the woman is of little consequence. Indeed, you have more present concerns to be thinking of."

John sat back into the chair again, chewing his lower lip, his brows knit, a petulant expression on his face – *like that of a thwarted child*, Giles thought scornfully.

Eleanor ignored his glowering expression. "So what of the device, de Soutenay?"

"I spoke with the woman, Madame. She was for certes no nymph. Neither was she a sorceress."

Eleanor tutted impatiently.

"Her grandsire is a Jewish healer, my lady."

A small hiss came from John. "A Jewess? She looked like no Jew to me."

"Her mother converted, married a Christian apothecary of her grandsire's acquaintance."

Lie was following upon lie as Giles tried to build a believable story. A slight sweat sheened his brow, and he hoped he didn't look as desperate as he felt. The story was thin enough, but he couldn't think of any way to make the events of the last day or so believable. Hell's teeth! He barely believed it himself. He swallowed again and continued. "The old man forgave his daughter; she was his only child. And he is right fond of his granddaughter, is teaching her his craft."

"I think I should meet this apothecary," John said. "And, indeed, why exactly was this Jewish apothecary's granddaughter visiting the good Abbess of Sparnstow?"

Giles groaned inwardly. He was starting to get tangled in his own web now. He had known convincing John would be no easy task. Indeed, without Eleanor's unexpected intervention, things would have been even more difficult. It would be wise to try and avoid too many twisted threads. Mayhap if he could keep their attention focussed on the device, they would become less interested in Marion.

"My lord, should it become known you were meeting with an apothecary, and a Jewish one at that, speculation would be rife." John opened his mouth, but Giles held up his hand. "Pray, allow me to continue. Apparently, the device can be used once only."

John's teeth showed, and he took a breath slowly, contemplatively. "There are more such of these devices?"

"Not as yet, my lord. Marion tells me more can be made, but they are difficult to fashion and the herbs used in them are rare and expensive, not growing in this country."

"Had you taken this woman into custody, I'll warrant her family would have procured them quickly enough," John snarled.

"I must confess, de Soutenay, I am, for once, in agreement with my son," Eleanor remarked.

"Not so, my lady. Marion assures me her grandsire travels to foreign domains to acquire them, and the secret of blending them is known only to him and to Marion's father. But they are loyal subjects of the crown and want only what is best for you, Sire. It will be their honour to serve you by providing you annually with these devices, for the herbs contained within last but a year."

"Hmm. Annually. Like a tax. Yes, the idea pleases me." John leaned forward again, one elbow on his knee, eyes narrowed, hand stroking his neat beard. "But can I trust them?"

"My liege, their desire is to serve you, but this needs to be conducted with the utmost secrecy. Not only are the devices rare and valuable–"

"So why am I not to meet these paragons of virtue?" John's tone was becoming silky, a bad sign.

Giles swallowed hard, wishing he was anywhere but here. The confines of the room seemed to be growing smaller by the minute, and he felt as though he was wearing a noose about his neck. "Sire, they would be honoured to meet with you, but if it became known that they serve you in this way, both your and their own lives would be put at risk. It would be easier, by far, for your enemies to deal with them than you, and then all would be lost. You have many enemies, and there are those who serve you who would not hesitate to betray you. Is that not so?"

"It grieves me to agree with you, de Soutenay, but certainly there are those who serve me who cannot be trusted." John gave a sidelong glance at Eleanor. "I feel sure, ma Mère, that yours are not the only spies at court. And so," he focussed his gaze on Giles again, "how do you propose to acquire this wondrous device, de Soutenay?"

"My liege, Marion has given me her word that I may collect it from her over Whitsuntide."

John stiffened. "Whitsuntide? A strange date to acquire it. Indeed, to meet with this woman on such a day has the feel of sorcery about it. Are you sure there is no taint of witchcraft here?"

Eleanor gave him a disdainful look and spoke with asperity. "I think we would do better not to enquire into certain things. And, my son, if some are to be believed, I, myself, am descended from Melusine." Her eyes crinkled with amusement, "Indeed, many of your father's advisers would have sworn an oath on it." She paused. "John, my son, it seems you have need of this device whether or no witchcraft is involved. And indeed, Whitsuntide is a most auspicious and holy time. Mayhap we should consider it a benison from our blessed Lord himself. Perhaps," she mused, "it might be considered as miraculous as Barnacle Goose."

Giles and John both smirked. Barnacle Goose was an excuse used to eat meat on a day of fasting. Considered to be fish, not flesh, few people actually believed it, but it made a good argument for varying the dull Lenten fare.

"And it does not seem at all strange to me that our Lord should provide a miraculous cure on such a day. Besides," she said, looking at them sharply, "miracle or other, you need this device. De Soutenay is in the right of it; you must not be seen to have any connection with this apothecary or his family. De Soutenay," she purred, favouring Giles with a smile which was almost bewitching in itself, "it is only to be expected that you might go missing around then, to have, let us say, a dalliance with some wench. I feel sure you understand me. We shall expect your reappearance right speedily, however. And no more shall be said about this device outside of we three."

Eleanor gazed at him speculatively. "If you are faithful in this matter, you shall be recompensed right well. It is high time you were wed. I shall cast my eyes around for a suitable heiress for you. No doubt I can convince the King that you are deserving of this favour, having served my will so faithfully. No, of *course*, I shall not tell Richard what service he has provided, John.

"Know you, de Soutenay, that Richard would not refuse me this boon, so long as I choose an heiress whom he has not already selected for disposal."

Giles felt a small frisson of relief. He knew any heiress provided would not be one of the wealthiest young women at the crown's bestowment, but certainly, if he could perform this well, he would keep his lands, be able to add to them and have Eleanor's protection, which was not something he took lightly. He just hoped this heiress would be young and well-favoured; it was not always the case. Still, he was in no position to be choosy. As long as she was not past her prime and had lands to add to his own, he would accept her gratefully.

"Now," Eleanor continued, "I shall leave this matter in your hands, and if you should happen to be about your own business for the next sennight or more, and if you should happen to keep a secret tryst with a young woman, I am sure we would need no knowledge of the details. Only," she paused, her pointed chin resting on her slender hand, "be very certain not to tarry longer than necessary. I am sure I do not need to remind you not to disappoint us. Now," she waved her hand in elegant dismissal, "for certes you wish to refresh yourself." She gestured that the audience was at an end. Giles rose to his feet, executed a somewhat stiff bow, for he had been long on horseback that day, and removed himself hastily from their presence.

Reaction set in almost immediately. The knots forming in his muscles tightened, and he almost stumbled as he made his way to the great hall.

Glancing around, he saw only wine. *Faugh!* He needed something lighter, more refreshing.

"Hoy, Will." He gestured to one of the younger squires. "Ale, and that right quickly."

He seized the ale the squire brought him and tossed most of it back in two swallows, leaning against the wall while his erratic heartbeat slowed to its usual pace. Not for a dozen heiresses would he go through that again. Clammy with sweat, he felt as exhausted as at the end of a hard battle. Thank heaven he had eaten at a hostelry on the way here; for of a surety, he could force down nothing more solid than this for the nonce. He took another swig and immediately choked, as a rough clout on his shoulder made him stagger. Making an obscene remark, he turned to see his elder brother at his elbow.

"You look as though a goose walked over your grave, little brother. I swear you are almost greensick." Ralph de Soutenay guffawed and buffeted him jovially again. Giles smiled thinly, not in the mood for his brother's boisterous humour.

"It's far too long since you warmed yourself at our hearth, Giles." The honeyed tones of Maude, Ralph's wife, met his ear. He saw her standing just behind Ralph, slender and elegant in her court dress of blue with silver stitchery round the neck and hem. God send him an heiress as fair.

Maude stepped forward, raised herself on tiptoe and kissed him warmly on the cheek. "Time you saw your godson again. Will you not pay a visit to us soon, if John can spare you?"

A visit to his brother's manor, which stood a scant ten miles from Sparnstow, would prove to be the perfect cover. It would certainly be pleasant company, and he was grateful to be able to remove himself from the poisonous atmosphere at court. He put a careless arm around Maude's slim waist, kissed her soundly and nodded his assent. "That can be arranged. I'll warrant young Martin has grown a handspan since I last saw him."

Giles smiled. It couldn't have worked better had he planned it himself.

CHAPTER FOURTEEN

2006

As the girls clambered into the car, I glanced at my watch. Only 5 pm? Surely not. I felt as though I had been gone for hours. Maybe things had happened more quickly in that other world. Certainly, a lot had been packed into what now seemed to be a scant space of time. I had no idea what hour I'd arrived in the past; couldn't even remember what time we'd arrived at the Abbey. We'd stopped on the way there for an early lunch, but I seemed to have completely lost track of time, and I suppose it would be impossible to tell if the clocks matched up exactly. Come to that, did they have clocks back then? How were they able to tell the time at all?

The girls chatted behind me, both opting to sit in the back seat so they could spread out their treasures. It looked to me as though they had bought half the contents of the gift shop.

"Did you enjoy it?" I called over my shoulder.

"Yes! It was so cool. Mum, you should see what we've got. We've got maps and charts of what it looked like before horrid old Henry had it destroyed. It was beautiful." Chloe heaved a big sigh of satisfaction. "Just imagine. I can't wait to show you."

That would be interesting. I must remember not to look as though I actually knew any of it already. "So would you have liked to live back then?"

"Yes!"

"NO!"

Shannon's "No!" was even louder than Chloe's "Yes."

"Oh, Shannon, you would. It would have been lovely." Chloe was determined to instil her own yearnings into her sister.

"No, it wouldn't. I'd have been married to some horrid old man, or I'd have been a boring old nun, or I might even have been poor and lived in a hovel."

I smirked. Shannon's streak of practicality would always come to the fore. To say she was prosaic would have been an understatement, but she had a point.

"I wouldn't have been poor." Chloe clung to her dreams determinedly. "I'd have been rich, I just know it. I'd have had beautiful gowns, and I'd have married a young, handsome knight and lived in a castle."

I drove them home arguing happily. It seemed only too likely that life in twelfth century England would have been no bed of roses, whether you were rich or poor.

"Mum?"

"Yes, Shannon."

"You know when you fell over under that tree?"

"Yep." I kept my eyes on the road; we were nearly home, but there was a tricky roundabout coming up ahead.

"I thought I heard a swarm of bees."

I indicated frantically and swerved into a layby.

"Muuuuum! What was that for?"

"Sorry, girls." I grasped at a straw. "Something just flew into the car and went down my neck. It's all right, Shannon," as she shrieked, "it wasn't a bee. I think it was a ladybird. It's tickling me, and I couldn't concentrate on the road." I wriggled and scratched convincingly, whilst trying to digest what Shannon had said. If anyone had heard the tree, I would have thought it would have been imaginative Chloe, not my steady, down-to-earth little Shannon.

"Bees?" I said, trying to keep my voice steady. "Really? Did you hear them, Chloe?"

"Course not. There wasn't a single bee anywhere. I would have noticed," she said virtuously.

I got a grip, steadied my nerves and turned the engine back on. Shaken, I slipped back into the

142

traffic, trying to focus. There was too much on my mind for conversation, and I drove home in silence, tormented by what I'd heard. I hoped this time travelling wasn't some kind of awful gift which I could pass on to her. Frowning, I shook my head impatiently. *Don't be stupid.*

When we got home, I was too busy to think on the day's events further, but that evening, after dinner, Chloe insisted on watching something she'd found about medieval times on the TV. Normally, I'd have chatted with Tom or read a magazine, or something; this time, I watched avidly. It wasn't the twelfth century; it was about Alfred the Great, whoever he was. I was disappointed, but despite myself, I found it fascinating. I found I had to stop myself making comments.

Chloe sat there, transfixed; Shannon was texting. I snuggled up against Tom, and he put an arm round me.

"What happened to you today, then? Did you see a ghost at the Abbey or something?"

I pulled away and looked at him, feeling a flush rise up my neck. "What do you mean?"

He laughed. "I've never seen you interested in this sort of thing before. That trip to the Abbey must have been good."

Relieved, I just nodded and leaned back against him. Then, my eyes went back to the TV, but my concentration was gone. I was just beginning to remember I had a promise to keep, and I didn't have much time. There was nothing I could do tonight though. Luckily, I was booked off work next week. Tom and I were redecorating the kitchen, but Tom would be doing most of the work. He didn't really appreciate my painting skills, so I would be prepping and clearing up. There would be plenty of time for me to do research in between. I scratched at a bite on my neck absentmindedly. *Darned gnats.*

The programme finished, Chloe switched off the TV and turned around, her eyes shining. "Wasn't that great?" She grabbed at my hand mid-scratch and stared with avaricious eyes at the heavy gold ring Hildegarde had given me. "Wow. What have you got there, Mum? That's just awesome. Can I try it on?"

"Sure." I tugged it off and threw to at her. "Catch."

She fumbled at it for a second then dropped it.

"Butterfingers." Tom chuckled.

"No, I'm not. I caught it, but it gave me a shock. It must have got static electricity or something." She rubbed at her hand. "Take it back, Mum."

I reached out for it, but Shannon got there first. I paused, hand still outstretched, horrified at the expression on her face. Shannon didn't like stuff like this, preferring dainty things with butterflies, but suddenly, I was looking at a stranger. She held it in her hand, turning it, examining it. Then, she slid it on her thumb and held her hand out to admire it. Her face took on shadows that had nothing to do with the lamp she was sitting beneath; her eyes were fixed. Suddenly, she wrenched it off and gave it back to me. "It's yours. You should wear it, it isn't mine yet."

I slid it back on my finger; it felt smooth, comforting. She was right, it *was* mine.

Tom took my hand, assessing it. "Nice," he said. "Looks like a man's ring to me. And it looks like it's worth a few quid. Where did you get it?"

I looked him straight in the eyes. "A ghostly abbess gave it to me." He grinned. "Honestly, Tom, you wouldn't believe me if I told you."

Shannon kept her eyes on my face. "I'm tired, I'm going to bed. Coming Chloe?"

As they went out the door, Shannon turned and looked at me intently. "I did hear bees," she said quietly. "I know there weren't any, but I did hear them."

CHAPTER FIFTEEN

I'd done it. It had been far easier than I had expected. Not that I could guarantee it would be any good; anything bought without a prescription on the internet is never without risk. But there they were, on the screen in front of me – epinephrine injectors. *Better get him a spare*, I supposed reluctantly. But oh, the price! If it wasn't for the fact that it might affect my future, he could have managed with just the one. But wait – that was in dollars. What would it be in pounds? I checked the currency convertor. Yeah, that sounded a bit more like it. It was still pretty steep though, a drain on our finances I didn't need. What a good job I was the one who did the family accounts. I wouldn't have wanted to try to explain to Tom.

I tried to imagine how I would react if things had been the other way round and he was telling me he'd travelled through time and met Prince John. Yeah, right! I'd have thought he was winding me up, that or going crazy. It wasn't really very believable, was it? The girls might have swallowed it; at their ages, beliefs were not so set in stone, and wanting to believe was half the battle, but even then…

I rubbed my garnet ring, remembering the expression on Shannon's face when she first saw it. That was my biggest concern. Somehow, Shannon *knew* something. She'd believe my story, not that she was ever going to hear it from me. Thank goodness Chloe had seen and heard nothing. And as for the ring, that was really strange. It seemed to repel her, in fact, which was just as well. Shannon was my sensible one. The thought of her ever ending up back there was enough to worry about. The idea of Chloe, with her head full of dreams, ever getting through that darned old beech, was enough to scare me to death. Shannon, at least, wouldn't go looking for adventures. I could only hope it would never draw her as it had me. I was sure of one thing; I was never taking either of them to Sparnstow, or within a twenty mile radius of it, ever again.

Coming back to what I was doing, I added two injector pens to my basket, crossed my fingers and paid up with a grimace. I hoped this site was genuine. It seemed the most likely. I'd actually been quite surprised how many places sold the things, along with all sorts of other medication. I never thought I'd be trying to buy anything without prescription. Still, at least it wasn't something illegal. Now, I just had to hold my breath and hope the dratted things showed up. I only had a couple of weeks. If they didn't come, what would I do? And what would poor Giles do?

It was funny, I didn't think when I was shrinking from that terrible sword or hissing threats at him, that I'd ever come to think of him as 'poor Giles.' If I'd had a dagger on me, I really do think I might have stabbed him. I'm not sure. I don't think I could ever stab someone anywhere vital, but if it was a case of that or being taken prisoner, who knows? But as I came to see the very real strain he was under, he got beneath my guard. And somehow, it seems strange to think it, but we had made some kind of connection. I almost felt as though part of him was in my blood.

I shook my head to dispel my thoughts, closed down the computer and got to my feet. Tom and I had finished most of the decorating last week, but there were still some tasks to be done. As I only worked part-time, I was tackling them. Leaving the past behind me, I pushed my hair behind my ears, put on my overalls and got to work.

The Wednesday before Whitsun, nothing had arrived. No injectors. As the day wore on and no deliveries appeared, my nerves were stretched to breaking point. I couldn't sit still, couldn't concentrate. The girls had both been at home since Monday with stomach bugs. Nearly recovered now, they were mostly glued to the TV or their mobiles, thank goodness, but even they noticed I was on edge.

That night, lying next to Tom, I looked out of the window, wide awake. Finally, after a couple of hours trying not to fidget, I must have nodded off, when I was woken by the sound of a tractor. Wait! Tractor? It was still dark. The sound started up again. Tom! Of all the times for him to start snoring. He hardly ever did. I nudged him in the ribs, and he turned over. I tried to settle down again, but I was wide awake now. Maybe I'd get myself a hot drink and read for a while. It might help me to relax. Slipping quietly out of bed, I put on my dressing gown and padded from the room.

Just making a cup of cocoa helped steady me. If they didn't come, then they didn't come. There was nothing I could do. And for goodness sake! Giles had been dead for centuries. Oh! I shuddered, and it wasn't the cold. Why did that thought have to come into my head now? The man who had kissed me – nothing but bones in his tomb. Horrible! And Hildegarde too. All that life and energy. Was there life after death? Hildegarde obviously believed it, I wished I did too. Maybe I'd read my Bible sometime. Did they have Bibles in those days? Surely the nuns did. If ever I met her again, I'd have to ask her what she did believe. If ever...but then that wasn't going to happen. Even if the goods arrived on time, I was only putting them through the beech. No way was I going back there. I used to think England was going to hell in a handcart, but that was before I'd had a sword held at my heart by a man in a mail shirt in the twelfth century. At least we have laws now; there seemed to be precious few back then. I picked up a magazine and tried to concentrate on that, sipped at my cocoa and then curled up on the sofa and slept.

The shrill of the doorbell jolted me awake, and I blinked blearily at the clock; Tom must have slipped out to work without disturbing me. A thud came from overhead. Chloe! I had to reach the door before she did. If that was my delivery, she wouldn't stop to see who it was addressed to – not Chloe. If she was given a parcel, she'd tear into it straight away, and how would I explain it? Leaping from the sofa and pulling my dressing gown around me, I flew to the door, reaching it just in time. Chloe hovered behind me, peering over my shoulder, trying to see what I was signing for.

"It's for me. Go on; go back to bed, and I'll bring you up a cup of tea." She lingered, looking at the package in my hand expectantly. "Go on. I'll be up in a moment."

Walking into the kitchen, I shut the door behind me. My hands shook as I tore the box open. As the injectors came into sight, I realised I'd been holding my breath and exhaled in a rush. They looked all right. I picked one up and examined it more closely. Nothing seemed to be amiss. What about the use by date? Yup. That was all right too. They would last until next year. As for the epinephrine they contained – who knew? We'd have to hope they would work well enough if they were ever needed.

Slipping the box into my denim bag, I tucked it into the cupboard, turned on the kettle and suddenly remembered something. Hildegarde! Didn't she say she really missed tea? If it wasn't for Hildegarde, who knows what would have happened to me? I would have been half crazed with fear, maybe never have got back to my own time. I owed her. Smiling to myself, I took a packet of loose tea and tipped it into an empty caddy. I'd love to be able to see her face when she tasted her first cup of tea in thirty years.

CHAPTER SIXTEEN

3rd June 1191
Whit Monday

Well before dawn some three weeks later, while most were still sleeping, Giles slipped quietly into the stables at Ralph's manor at Oakley. A scurry and rustling came from the pile of straw on his right, and a grimy face with tousled hair peered up at him, blinking owlishly. "Sire?"

"Go back to your dreams, boy. I'll saddle Troubadour here myself."

The pale grey eyes looked startled.

"Don't look so surprised. If a man cannot saddle and bridle his own horse, then he should not be riding one." Giles' father had insisted his sons were competent at looking after their own mounts. The eyes blinked again at him in acquiescence, and the face disappeared back into the straw.

As he saddled Troubadour, the big horse pushed his nose insistently at Giles' tunic until he found one of the apples Giles had taken from the kitchen as he left. The sorrel whickered in satisfaction at him, and he absently fondled the swivelling ears, his mind on the day ahead. She would be there, would she not? His whole future depended on one woman. It was not something he relished, preferring to control his own destiny, not leave it to the whims of others. Despite his calm exterior, Giles' insides lurched slightly. He had bid farewell to Ralph and Maude last night; they knew he must be about his own business today. Maude had been wrath with him for leaving his nephew without a farewell – "Martin will be upset," she told him, hands on her hips. "Why could you not have mentioned it earlier?" And nothing would do but to wake the child and say his adieus, promising him a gift next time he came to call. Still, it meant he could leave before all were awake today, with no bad feelings. And mayhap he would not leave it so long next time. The boy was growing like a tadpole.

He added to his bags a pouch, which he had stuffed with food filched from the kitchens along with a costrel of ale and the apple Troubadour had just eaten. Giles was edgy now and eager to be on his way, and his mood communicated itself to Troubadour, who pranced impatiently. He pulled the tossing head down and murmured to him, "Hush now. No need to wake the whole household this early."

Leading the horse from the stable, he heard a muffled female squeal from the pile of straw into which the boy had disappeared. He grinned, realising the lad hadn't been alone under there – older than he looked then.

Troubadour picked his way through the countryside, ears twitching as birds started their exuberant dawn chorus. The sun began to tint the skies, and Giles felt himself begin to relax again. A pity he had to wear his gambeson and mail, but there was much unrest. A lone traveller was wise to be protected. It was a nuisance though, for even at this hour, the day was bidding fair to become over warm.

Troubadour snuffed the air and tossed his head. Giles gave him a friendly thwack. A man and his horse, what could be more pleasant?

A couple of hours or so later, he was within view of the Abbey. From this rise, he could see into the grounds, see the choir nuns filing from the chapel. Should he pay his respects to the Abbess? No, time enough for that later. He paused. A pity they hadn't thought to ask Marion whether she would return in the forenoon or later; he might have a long vigil ahead. Still, the day was pleasant enough for now, and better over hot than a cold, rain-sodden watch. And he was well provisioned.

It wasn't often he had an entire day to himself. Might it have been wise to request stabling for Troubadour at the Abbey? No, he thought not. The grass was plentiful; the horse may as well enjoy the day too.

Hildegarde left the Abbey chapel after Prime feeling slightly disordered. Something was nagging in the back of her mind. The soothing chant of the Divine Office had not been able to dislodge it nor bring it into submission. Indeed, she had found it hard to set her mind to her devotions at all.

As she walked across the courtyard to the lavatorium, she felt uneasy. *What is it, Lord? What am I missing?* She had not felt so disturbed for years. Her vocation, although it had been unexpected – *Unexpected? There was an understatement,* she smiled – had brought her a peace she had never expected to find. The young student she had been would never recognise the woman she was now. Contented, fulfilled. But today...oh, what was wrong with her? Even the joyous birdsong failed to gladden her heart. It was no good. She needed to seek peace. Having completed her ablutions and her private Mass, she decided to abstain from breaking her fast and turned back into the chapel. Kneeling before the altar, gazing in despair at her crucified Lord, she bowed her head and sought refuge in her prayers. She stayed there until her knees were sore, but still, she felt a tug in the corner of her mind. What was it? What was this feeling of unease? Crossing herself, she rose creakily to her feet and went thoughtfully to the Chapter Mass. The glory of the early summer morning was lost on her, the melodic chorus of the blackbird no more than a cacophony of distraction.

All morning, Hildegarde's thoughts whirled in a disorderly swarm. After High Mass, deciding to fast through dinner, she asked her prioress to take her place in the refectory and sat distracted in her chambers, elbows on her desk, chin resting on her hands, eyes gazing at some point far beyond. A tap at the door roused her. "Come."

Ursel peered round the door at her, concern in the depths of her hazel eyes.

"God's blessing, Sister. You have need of me?" Hildegarde started to rise as the elderly nun came into the room bearing a tray with bread, cheese and a cup of ale.

"Mother Abbess, you missed your meal. You will be hungered." Ursel put the tray firmly down before the Abbess and bade her eat.

Hildegarde turned rueful eyes on her. "And what if I were fasting, Sister Ursel?"

"Dear Mother Abbess, plenty of time for that on days when we are bidden to do so, but when you need all your wits about you, it is no time to be fasting. Have you remembered what day it is?"

A flash of clarity struck Hildegarde so hard that she sat down abruptly in her chair, causing Ursel to tut in concern. "No, Sister Ursel, I am not feeling faint. Now, I know what it is that has been nagging at me like a toothache. Bless you, Sister. You have brought me more than sustenance; you have brought me enlightenment. Won't you sit and share this with me? I have need of your opinions to help me order my thoughts."

The wrinkled old face lit up. Ursel always enjoyed time with Mother Abbess. Why, she remembered the strange young maid who had first joined their order and the odd tale she had to tell. Lucky it had been Ursel who had come across her that day, lying there in the grass by that old beech tree, addled out of her wits. Lucky too that Abbess Matilda, who reigned supreme when Ursel had been but a novice, was gone. In her reign, Hildegarde would have been suspected of madness, such strange things she had spoken. But Matilda had been superseded by the time Hildegarde had appeared at the Abbey by a gentler abbess, gifted with an open mind and a kinder rule. Between them, they had pieced together the truth of her arrival. And oh, how her presence had been ordained! Such an outbreak of fever and vomiting there had been soon after that. Ursel was already infirmaress, but her skills, though as good as any apothecary, were inadequate for so many patients, her sister nuns worn to the bone and falling ill with the sickness themselves. Hildegarde, with her unheard of knowledge of medicine and nursing from the future and her calm demeanour, had turned the tide of the sickness. Her ideas had been so unfamiliar to them. How they had balked. How they had remonstrated with her. But she had reasoned with them – explaining, showing, teaching. As even more nuns fell ill, it had seemed worth trying anything. And it had worked. No new cases, and those who had seemed on the brink of death had been pulled back to this life. And the girl had been blessed with a vocation, stayed and now, in turn, blessed the sisters with a reign which was as wise as it was good. Ursel said a prayer of thanks as she broke bread with Hildegarde, frowning as Hildegarde clapped a hand to her forehead, exclaiming, "Oh, what a fool I am!"

"Abbess?"

"I told her Whit Monday. How could I have been so stupid?"

"Stupid? Why, Mother Abbess, what do you mean?"

"How could I have forgotten? How will she know what date it is in our time? And even if she does realise, it will not avail her."

"Realise?" Ursel was baffled.

"Ursel, the dates change! *The date of Whitsun changes each year.*" She rested her head on her hands and let out a groan. "That poor young man. He will think she has forgotten him. He'll believe she betrayed him. *And he will have nothing to give to John.* Oh, how could I have been so stupid?"

Ursel quite forgot she was speaking to her Abbess, going to her side, putting an arm round her and soothing her as she would a patient. "Never fret, sweeting, we will find a way. Come now, calm yourself. Let us put our heads together and see if we cannot resolve this. Come now, come now," she comforted the distraught Abbess. "As it is, it has not gone beyond what can be mended. Calm yourself, and let us see what can be done."

Hildegarde wiped a tear from her eye with a scrap of linen. Ursel was right. All was not lost. Whatever had come over her? She sat up straight, gave the old woman a grateful smile and set her mind to the subject.

"Now," continued Ursel, "I daresay that young knight has already started on his journey. Like as not, he'll be tethering that fine horse of his near the beech about now. But what if Marion does not return today? It is no great matter. We shall set aside a guest chamber here at the Abbey, and he may stay here until she comes. For she will come. That was a young woman who could be trusted. I could see it in her. I daresay John will not make great bones about a day or so either way. That's if de Soutenay survived the telling of whatever tale he finally concocted – and I hope it was a good one!"

Hildegarde relaxed. Ursel was in the right of it. She put out her hand and covered the wrinkled claw of the old infirmaress. "What a blessing you have been to me this morning, Sister. I confess, my senses have been quite disordered. But you are correct. All we need to do is get word to Giles. Now, how shall we accomplish that?"

Ursel grinned. "Brother Bernard would find it a great pleasure. You know how he loves to help, and he is so stolid, has no imagination whatsoever. Nothing would ever convince him Marion was a wood nymph, whether she stepped through the tree before his very eyes or even descended from the heavens or rose out of the earth. He would surely find some reasonable explanation."

Hildegarde almost laughed to picture the scene. But again, Ursel was right. He was the very man. She would send him to watch over Giles from a distance. If nothing had happened when dusk started to fall, then Bernard should bring him to the Abbey where she could speak to him.

"Sister Ursel, may God bless you, you have quite restored me. We shall request Sister Hosteller to prepare a chamber at once."

"Ah, as to that, 'twasn't me who restored you; 'twas that good bread and cheese. To say nothing of the ale."

CHAPTER SEVENTEEN

Now he had arrived at the beech, the sun was beginning to feel uncomfortably warm on his mail. Giles wished there was at least one more tree in the vicinity for shade and to lean against. Still, there was no help for it. He sat himself down on the tussock he had tripped over last time, eyes fixed firmly on the tree. For the first hour or so, nerves on the raw with expectation, he started each time an insect buzzed past, thinking the magic was beginning.

After half a dozen such starts, his tension began to ease, and he felt his stomach starting to growl. Pulling out one of the meat pasties he had brought with him to fortify himself, he bit into it hungrily. Doubtless, she would arrive sometime between now and dusk.

As the sun reached its zenith, the heat blazed down onto his hauberk. Sweat started to soak the heavy gambeson, despite the surcoat he had worn to shield himself, and Giles wished he had been less cautious in his preparation. He swore silently.

If any enemies came upon him now, all they would have to do was wait for him to broil to death in his own juices. A pity the only shade was that cast by the beech.

He was tempted to move back from the clearing and sit in the shadow afforded by the trees at the edge of the wood but afraid to stray that far from his trysting place. And to venture closer to the beech would be an act of recklessness. He had left Troubadour tethered loosely within reach of the stream, knowing that, should felons attempt to touch him, they would be at risk of hooves and teeth. Troubadour was a one-man horse. Besides, the creature would be more comfortable there. Giles only wished he had the same comforts.

Wiping the perspiration from his face with the back of his hand, he swore again before pulling out a costrel of ale, removing the stopper with his teeth and taking a hefty swig.

If he stayed here in the sun, he would surely roast. He took another pasty, chewing absently as he pondered his options. The shade of the beech extended far enough from its trunk to make him consider taking the risk.

Giles inched forward cautiously until he reached the edge of the shade. It was still hot but better, for sure, than sitting in the full glare of the day. He ate the last mouthful of pasty almost without noticing, and then wished he had savoured it more. Pulling out an apple, he bit into it, not taking his eyes from the tree. Then, tossing the core away, he pulled up one knee, leaned his arm on it and waited. And waited. The heat of the sun continued its relentless assault and, slowly, his head began to droop.

Giles let out a sudden snort and awoke with a jerk. The sun was no longer directly overhead, the shade had lengthened. How long had he been asleep? He cursed his stupidity. He would have had a man flogged for falling asleep on duty. Now, he shook himself angrily to full wakefulness. Had he missed her?

Standing up stiffly, he arched his spine, then, with some misgivings, moved closer to the tree, head cocked to one side, listening for the slightest sign of humming and ready to leap backwards if he felt a pull.

No buzz. He edged closer, eyes fixed on the hollow at the base of the trunk. Mayhap she had delivered the device while he had been sleeping. An unexpected feeling of disappointment swept over him, and he scolded himself. What point in seeing her again anyway? It was not as though there could be a future for them. Nevertheless, the sense of loss could not be shaken.

Ah well, naught for it but to retrieve the device and be on his way.

He knelt and reached out his hand cautiously; he had no wish to be sucked from his own life, whatever the marvels Marion's time held. Ignoring the prickling sensation at the base of his scalp, he pushed one hand into the hollow and felt around. Nothing! Throwing caution to the wind, he thrust his other hand into the hollow, scrabbling in disbelief as a sick feeling of dread swept over him. There was nothing there.

He had let down his guard, trusted her – and she had defaulted.

Regardless of the risk now, he thrust his hands deeper beneath the roots of the tree, groping frantically. So intent was he on his task that, when a large hand came down upon his shoulder, he nearly jumped from his skin. An obscene oath died on his lips as he turned, only to see a heavy-set lay brother from the Abbey standing over him, face full of concern. Giles' eyes widened in disbelief for behind the monk, nibbling unconcernedly at the grass, stood Troubadour.

"Hellfire! How came you to go near my horse without losing an arm? Is everyone in this abbey possessed of witchcraft?"

The brother's large face creased into an apologetic smile. "Sire, beg pardon for startling you. My Abbess would speak with you privately. She bade me come."

His eyes crinkled with embarrassment. "She…er, she…told me to…to guard the tree for you." It sounded right silly to Brother Bernard, but if that was what the Abbess required, it was not his place to argue. "See, I have brought your horse for you."

He turned to the horse, speaking soft words as he scratched a spot on Troubadour's withers. The horse snorted ecstatically and leaned his weight against Bernard, who braced himself.

Giles watched in fascination. "Are you a sorcerer? My horse goes with no man of his own free will."

When Brother Bernard stopped scratching, Troubadour whickered in protest and nuzzled at his shoulder. One large hand went back to his withers and resumed its task; the big horse snorted blissfully.

"I fancy I have a way with horses," Bernard said. "The pity is, most of 'em are too small to seat me." An expression of wistfulness flickered across his face and was gone. "Of course, there's not much call for a man of my persuasion to ride now, but ah, when I was younger!"

Giles recalled himself to the task in hand. "You say the Abbess would speak with me?"

"Aye. Quickly now, make haste. And I daresay you wish for some victualling for you and the horse as well. It will be provided at the Abbey."

Giles glanced at the tree.

"Don't you be worrying yourself about yonder tree, I'll stay to watch it. Though who is going to move it, I can't imagine. It looks secure enough to me." Brother Bernard handed the reins to Giles, who wasted no more time in discussion. Swinging himself up onto Troubadour's broad back and leaving the lay brother staring in puzzlement at the tree, he rode disconsolately to the Abbey. Whatever the Abbess had to say, it could do naught to lift his spirits.

A cloud came, as though from nowhere, and shadowed the sun. It brought no welcome relief for Giles, merely emphasised the darkness overshadowing his soul.

The porteress had evidently been watching as the gate was opened before him, and another lay brother was waiting to stable his horse. Dismounting, he stroked Troubadour's nose and handed him over to the care of the brother. Troubadour went willingly; it was only when men tried to lay hands on him without his master's consent that they discovered his temper.

Giles thought Sister Berthe had not yet forgiven him for his initial treatment of her, for she sniffed disdainfully as she escorted him, unsmiling, through the cloisters to the Abbess's chamber. As he entered the room, Hildegarde got to her feet, a smile of welcome on her face, Sister Ursel at her side, both looking a sight more pleased to see him than had Sister Berthe.

Unmoved by their greetings, Giles looked despondently at the two women, his stomach in his boots.

"My dear de Soutenay." The Abbess held both hands out to him. He ignored them.

"My lady, I'll not be taking up your time. I'll
head to France, offer my sword to the French
King." His voice was grim. "I've no choice. My life
won't be worth a groat once John finds out I've not
procured the device. If I might have a chamber for
the night and stabling for Troubadour, I'll be gone
'ere it's light. No need for John to take his temper
out on you if he knows not that I've involved you.
I've farewells to make to my brother and little time
to waste." He turned from them, wanting nothing
more than to sit in the silence of the guest chamber
and drink himself into a stupor. And if that was
wrong, he knew of many an abbot who regularly
did likewise.

"My lord, wait!" The clear voice arrested him
and he hesitated, one hand on the latch.

"For what?" he said bleakly. "I've nothing to stay
for now. I put my life in Marion's hands. For
whatever reason, she either couldn't or wouldn't
return. My life here is done, and there's an end to
it."

"*No*! Please, stay. Let me explain." Hildegarde
almost ran to stand between Giles and the door. "I
made an error."

"As did I."

"Sir Giles, *think*! What do you know about
Whitsuntide? Or rather, what do you *not* know
from year to year?"

He looked at her impatiently, wanting only to be
alone, to hide his defeat from these well-

intentioned women. "My lady, with all respect, I've no time for such riddles."

"This is no riddle. It is the reason she did not come – yet."

A flicker of hope rose in him. He let go of the door and turned back to her, a query in his eyes.

"Sir Giles, Whitsuntide is *variable*! It has no set date from year to year."

His heart lifted as enlightenment dawned. "It may be on a different date in Marion's time?"

"Precisely. She may not have let you down. It may not yet *be* Whit Monday in her time, even if the date there is the same here, and we cannot be sure of that."

The flicker of hope started to flare into a flame. "You mean…?" He hardly dared believe it.

"Yes! If it was on an earlier date in her time, the device would have already been there for you, and it wasn't, was it?" He shook his head. "Therefore, in her time, Whitsun *hasn't yet happened*."

Giles sat with a thud onto a settle beside the door. *As well that was padded,* he thought, landing heavily. *A fine bruise I'd have had on my rump if not.*

"So…?"

"All you need do is wait. Come back each day, or remain at the Abbey should you wish. We can prepare you a chamber. She'll be here; I'm sure of it, if not in the next week, then no later than the week after. Trust me." She put her hand on his arm. "You've had a long and fruitless day, Sir Giles. Our hosteller, Sister Joan, has already prepared you a chamber. You'll find all you need there, a ewer, food and wine. Rest tonight, at least."

"My thanks, I'll stay tonight and be right grateful. It's not worth the trouble to travel back and forth from Oakley each day and would require too many explanations." His eyes crinkled with amusement. Maude was not a woman to scent a mystery without wanting to find out more. "I'll ride out to the beech again tomorrow. I confess, I am a happier man now than I was an hour ago. You've..." He flashed a grin at them as he remembered something. "What is it Marion said? You've blown my mind."

Hildegarde muffled a snort of laughter as she caught the expression on Ursel's face. The elderly nun looked as though her mind had indeed been blown, her face a picture of bewilderment. "A private joke, Sister," she explained. "And now, we must prepare to attend Compline. Sir Giles, we shall bid you goodnight and pray for a good outcome on the morrow."

As if in answer to an unspoken summons, there came a tap at the door, which opened to reveal Sister Joan, small and bustling. "Mother Abbess, I came to escort Sir Giles to his chamber."

She turned to him and indicated. "You'll remember the way, my lord. There's water laid out for you, and some wine and simple fare." Her footsteps and his faded as she led him away.

Hildegarde watched them for a moment then, her mind starting to focus on Compline, her spirit in communion with her Lord, she left her chambers and headed, with Ursel, to the Abbey chapel.

CHAPTER EIGHTEEN

4th June 2006
Whitsunday

It was Sunday night. I had laid my plans well. The girls had a treat arranged which was filling their heads to the exclusion of everything else. Tomorrow evening, Tom and I were taking them to a medieval banquet in London. "We'll hire costumes," I had told them. That wasn't good enough. At my words, two eager grins had transformed to down-drooped mouths.

"Oh Mum! Can't we buy them? They're really cheap online, and I want to keep mine."

"Well, I'm not dressing up." Tom had put his foot down. "You can all do what you like, but if I have to dress up, I'm not coming."

The girls had moaned a bit at Tom, but, anxious not to have the whole thing cancelled and pacified by being allowed to buy, not hire, had capitulated. To be honest, it made things easier for me, which – ahem – had been the reason I'd succumbed to their begging for this particular treat. I had my own reasons for wanting to get a medieval costume. Chloe and Shannon had chosen something that wealthy women might have worn. Not me.

Tomorrow morning, I was planning to pack my outfit in the basket Hildegarde had given me and take it to the beech. Maybe I could slip into it just before I put my hands through. I wasn't planning on going through again, but who knew what might go wrong? I certainly hadn't planned my last visit, so I had something plain and understated, just in case. If the worst happened, I wanted to attract as little attention as possible in either century. Neither Chloe nor Shannon was happy with my choice.

"Oh Mum, that's so boring! You'll look like our maid."

Exactly. Neither too rich nor too poor; it would suit me just fine.

Late that night, after the girls had gone to bed, my nerves started to kick in. Tom put his arm around me, and I snuggled up to him, trying to osmose some of his solid calmness into my veins. Not that he would have been calm himself if he had known what I would be up to tomorrow. I hugged him tightly and kissed him. My Tom.

"Love you," I murmured.

"Love you, too."

I hated not being able to confide in him, but he didn't seem to sense anything amiss in my manner. That's Tom. Steady, just like Shannon. You'd have to set fire to something under his nose for him to notice anything wrong.

He stood up, yawned and held out his hand. "Come on, Marion, let's hit the hay. Busy day tomorrow. I'm beat."

"You haven't forgotten I need you to keep an eye on the girls tomorrow morning, have you?"

"What?" He gaped at me, eyes wide, before bursting into laughter. "Only joking. Give your mum my love, and tell her we'll all come with you next time. C'mon." He switched off the light and headed up the stairs.

At least he would be able to sleep. He had nothing pressing on his mind, and my tossing and turning never seemed to disturb him. My own chances of getting a decent night were pretty slim. I found some herbal sleeping pills and knocked a couple back with a glass of milk. They weren't much good, but they might help.

I woke at 6:30 having slept in spite of my expectations, albeit fitfully. The herbal tablets had worked. I'd have to get some more.

Normally, I like to rouse slowly, but today, I was wide awake as soon as my eyes opened. Sliding out from between the covers, I crept to the bathroom, taking care not to wake the girls. I showered and dressed, then I packed my basket with care and left the house, shutting the door quietly behind me.

The morning was grey and overcast. Good! At this time, and on such a miserable day, the Abbey was not likely to be busy. The fewer people around, the better, as far as I was concerned. The traffic was light, and I made it to the Abbey before 8 am. It didn't even open until 10. With a bit of luck I'd have done what I needed to do and be long gone before the first visitors arrived. The car park was closed, but there were plenty of verges along that road.

5th June 1191

As the bell rang for Prime, and the nuns filed into the chapel, Giles mounted Troubadour and made for the beech. This would be his third day's vigil. Ursel and Hildegarde continued to reassure him Marion would come; he hoped they were right.

Yesterday had been mind-numbing, depressing. What little sleep he had last night had been filled with nightmares, and this morning, his eyes were heavy. He had been provided with bread, cheese and ale to sustain him today.

It had dawned overcast, damp and chill, and this time, he was grateful for the gambeson that had so plagued him previously. Brother Bernard had been given permission to accompany him to watch over Troubadour and was riding Horace, the Abbey's sway-backed nag, not a creature of beauty or grace but at least large enough that Bernard's feet were not dragging in the dust.

As the birds sang their paeans of praise, they rode at a steady trot towards the beech. This time, Giles tethered Troubadour near the stream, leaving Bernard to tend to him. The monk was obviously enjoying his spell as 'squire' and was murmuring soft words to Troubadour as Giles walked away. The horse wore that expression of bliss which indicated he was satisfied with the arrangements. Giles was beginning to wonder if, should Brother Bernard decide to mount him, instead of flinging him headfirst into the nearest bush, Troubadour would bear him meekly and quietly wherever he wished. *No, being entranced by the monk is one thing, allowing him to mount...*Giles shook his head. *Never.*

Bringing his mind back to the task in hand, he walked through the copse towards the beech, eyes fixed on the tree, until he had reached within a few feet of its spreading branches. Not taking his gaze from it, he spread his mantle on the dew-damp grass, sat himself down and waited.

Apart from the sporadic song of a mistle-thrush, nothing seemed to mark the passing of time. If Giles hadn't been so tense, he would have found the wait more tedious. Even so he felt as though he had been staring at the gnarled trunk for hours, almost afraid to look away. What if she was unable to get back? Or unable to procure the device? In his head, he had almost planned his route to France, planned the words with which he would offer his fealty to Philippe. It would be with reluctance. He may not want to work for John, but he was damned sure he didn't want to work for Philippe. His loyalties, his family ties, all were in England. *She must come. She must.*

He whiled away the time eating his bread and cheese, washing it down with ale, saving some for later, forcing himself to tear his gaze from the tree. Who knew how long he'd be keeping vigil? And all the time, his nerves were becoming more and more raw. He shook his head. His lack of sleep must be telling now, his head was buzzing. But wait! It wasn't his head. He looked up and saw the tree had started to shimmer. No heat haze this time. It must be Marion. She was coming.

Giles got to his feet, intending to move just close enough to reach out and touch Marion's hand when it appeared, but suddenly, an overwhelming urge came upon him. No man had ever seen beyond his own time, but here and now, he had the opportunity to see the future. Almost appalled at the thought, still he was unable to stop himself. The urge grew stronger and stronger, his head filled with the hum of a thousand bees. He drew ever closer to the beech. Against all his senses were telling him, he reached for the tree, watching as first his hand, then his arm disappeared. He felt his face drawn through the very fabric of the tree, as though he was pushing through something as thick as pottage. A mist was in his eyes. He blinked, and it started to clear. There she was, her face a mask of horror as she saw him. And beyond her – his jaw dropped in shock. The Abbey! What had happened to it?

CHAPTER NINETEEN

5th June 2006
Whit Monday

I parked the car. There wasn't a soul about. Good. I was wearing jeans today, slim fitting with a tight tee shirt. In my basket, I carried the outfit I had bought from the internet. I was not going to be caught unawares this time. As I hurried towards the tree, I kept looking furtively behind me; still no one in sight. Ducking behind the trunk, I pulled the outfit from my basket and slipped it over my jeans and top. It was a bit fiddly, and I struggled with the lacing, but I managed. Looking at the white scarf thingy – a wimple, Chloe had called it, hadn't she? – I tugged it over my hair and beneath my chin. Would it do? I hoped so.

I didn't know whether I could approach the tree from this side, so I went back around to roughly the same angle as before, but then moved back a few yards. I wasn't ready yet, didn't know if I dared. But I couldn't let Giles down, either.

Setting my teeth determinedly, I was about to start fumbling in my basket for the caddy and the auto-injectors when I felt the vibrations start. Not as intense as last time, but I supposed it was because this time I was coming to the tree of my own free will. Last time, I hadn't been. The hum started to resonate in my body again but not so unpleasantly this time. I squared my shoulders and got ready to approach the tree.

Wait! What was happening? The gnarled old trunk almost seemed to be wearing a face. My mouth dropped open in horror as the tree started to shimmer. It wasn't wearing a face; the face was coming through. It was Giles, his expression ghastly, as though he was staring at his own doom. But I was *not* letting this happen. It had been difficult enough for me to cope in his world. He was *not* coming through into mine. I sprinted to the tree just as his shoulders started to emerge, lunged at him, and we went tumbling back through, landing in a heap the other side.

For a few moments, we lay there winded. I was locked in a steel embrace, my body almost crushed against his mail, his arms around me, not in a lover's embrace, more a confused heap, the result of me hurling myself at him. My face pressed against his beard, the bristles grinding into my skin, his lips against my cheek, his breath warm on my skin.

Slowly, I recovered my wits. I started to lift myself, and he dropped his arms allowing me to roll off him. Sitting up, I wrapped my arms about my knees. He got to his knees, sat back on his heels, and for a moment, we just gazed at each other. His eyes looked haunted.

"Marion, the Abbey! It was in ruins. What happened?"

I shook my head. I didn't know. "It just fell into disrepair, I suppose. Oh, wait!" Could I tell him? He already knew more than he should. I supposed a little more information wouldn't hurt. It might help.

"I remember now. In a few hundred years' time…"

A look of utter confusion was in his eyes.

"In a few hundred years," I repeated, "there will be a king who disagrees with the Pope." I was glad I remembered that bit from school. It sounded about right. I'd have to check when I got back, but it wasn't as though anyone was going to tell him differently, except maybe Hildegarde. "He will overthrow religion as you know it now." He looked even more horrified. Maybe I shouldn't have told him, but it was too late to stop now. Perhaps I could soften the blow. I dredged up as much as I could remember from those long-ago history lessons. "It wasn't so bad. It meant everyone could believe in their own way eventually. And the Pope doesn't tell us what to do in England in my time.

He doesn't even tell the Italians what to do. Well," I amended, "he does, but they don't always take any notice. He hasn't the power in my time that he had in yours." Has, had? Which tense should I use? No matter. I wasn't taking an exam.

It wasn't helping. I could see him struggling to make sense of it all. "Giles, don't worry about it. It won't happen for hundreds of years yet."

"After I'm laid in the ground, you mean? Why do I not find that a comfort? It's just that…" he muttered, passing his hand across his eyes, "…when I looked into your world, I realised that to you, in your time, I'm entombed in my coffin. It's not a reassuring thought, Marion."

We sat in silence for a few moments, each digesting what the time gap really meant, before Giles spoke again. "And you – you're not even born. I cannot…it's just…" His voice tailed off.

Another thought hit me. My basket! The injectors. Were they still in one piece? I hoped the fall hadn't damaged them. As I turned to look for the basket, the same thought evidently occurred to him. He leaned forward and reached behind me. There it was. The basket was tumbled on its side, but the fabric cover was still in place. I pulled it off and looked inside. At least I'd had the forethought to wrap them in an old scarf. I took them out and examined them. They seemed none the worse.

"I think they'll be okay." He looked at me and I realised what I'd said. "I mean I think they are unbroken. They look as though they will still work." His face cleared. "And, Giles, I have a gift for the Abbess. It's in this caddy…er, this tin…er…never mind. It's in here. She'll know what it is. Tell her, if she gives you the caddy to replace with the unused devices each year, I will refill it for her." He took it from me along with the devices and put them in some kind of bag, a sort of large leather pouch.

It occurred to me that he had not noticed my more appropriate dress. I guessed that meant I'd got it right. He would have been more likely to comment if I had got it disastrously wrong.

We seemed not to be able to think of anything to say, were just sitting there in companionable silence. I had thought we would talk non-stop if we ever met again, but there didn't really seem to be any words which fitted. I should be going but felt a pang that I would never see him again. It's strange to speak to someone who is alive now but technically has been dead for hundreds of years. I wondered…

"How did it go with Prince John? Was he okay about things?"

"Okay?" Giles frowned as he repeated the unfamiliar word.

I kept forgetting he wouldn't understand me – this language gap was confusing. I tried again. "Er, was he agreeable to the plan? Did he cut up rough…I mean…"

"I think I can guess what you mean." He smiled. "'Cut up rough' seems a very apt description. In truth, I think my days might have been foreshortened had it not been for the Queen's intervention. That woman is remarkable. Mind you, I seem to be meeting any number of remarkable women of late."

"So are you to keep your lands?"

A ray of joy lit up his face. "Not only do I retain my lands, I am promised an heiress. Let us hope she will be young and beautiful too. Any amount of lands and wealth would not make up for being married to a shrew with no teeth or a horse-faced wench with a laugh to match."

I blinked. "But surely, you choose your own wife?"

He bared his teeth. "Not when the Queen has gone to the trouble of finding you an heiress. You smile gratefully and keep your tongue between your teeth. Then, you find consolation elsewhere."

"Oh." What else could I say?

He threw back his head and laughed. "Don't worry, sweeting. There is many a father anxious to please the Queen by offering his daughter. If I'm lucky, I'll get a sweet-faced virgin or a desirable young widow. As long as her looks aren't beyond redemption and her temper mild, I'm sure we'll be content enough. And if not, as I said, there is always consolation to be found."

I was a bit shocked by his pragmatic approach. Somehow, I'd assumed everyone in this day and age was religious. Maybe that was only in some respects. And I suppose if you don't get to choose your spouse, and you don't like them, you make the best of it. I wondered if it was the same for women of this era. Probably not.

He looked at me curiously. "From your speech, do I assume you chose your own man, and he you?"

"I certainly did. We marry whom we please in my time."

Those white teeth flashed again. "Now, that sounds passing pleasant to me."

I don't know how long we could have sat there, each fascinated to learn of the other's way of life, reluctant to part, but suddenly, a large horse came galloping through the trees, followed by a slightly smaller, shabbier mount. The larger of the two horses was ridden by the monk I had seen the previous time.

Giles' face took on a peculiar expression. "Brother, I assume you are riding Troubadour for a reason," he said, as the monk reached him, slid off and handed him the reins. "Indeed, I'm surprised you are able to ride him at all."

"No time for that, Sire, I came to warn you there's a party of horsemen approaching.

"Good day, my lady," he greeted me with a bob of his head, "and also farewell, for you need to leave now. You may borrow Horace if you have need of him." He indicated the second horse. "I'm sure the Abbess will understand."

"Thank you, Brother, but no, I won't need him." Would a horse even fit through? But there was no time to waste pondering on that. I needed to be through that tree before they appeared.

Giles turned and caught me in a brief hug. "Farewell Marion. I won't forget you."

"Nor I you."

"Now go, quickly."

He let me go and propelled me towards the beech. I didn't need telling twice. I held my breath and plunged through it, turning my head as I went to give one last wave as he and the monk faded before my eyes. The monk's expression of disbelief would stay with me a long time.

With a kind of plop, I stepped back into my own time, heart racing. I came out behind the tree this time, hidden from the Abbey grounds, and ripped off my medieval clothes not a moment too soon as a dog and its owner appeared on the other side of the field. I quickly thrust the garments into my basket. The dog, a heavy bloodhound, dashed up to me and jumped on my jean-clad legs, sniffing excitedly. I staggered beneath the onslaught but daren't lean against the tree. I wasn't going back again, and certainly not dressed like this.

"Down, Rufus! Get here!"

The dog ignored him and sniffed at me in some kind of olfactory delirium; maybe he could smell the past somehow. He was going crazy, slobbering and drooling on me then poking his nose into my basket and snuffling. His red-faced owner grabbed him by the collar and hauled him off, clipping him to his lead. "I'm so sorry, I don't know what's come over him. He never does this."

"No worries. I'll take it as a compliment."

He dragged the dog away, still apologising to me and cursing at it.

As for me, I was left feeling somehow bereft. It had all ended so suddenly, part of me seemed to be missing – left behind in the twelfth century. It is strange to have touched another world; maybe you leave something of your essence behind. I was surprised at the sense of loss. Of course, I hadn't left my heart behind; my heart was here, where it belonged, but still...

I sank down on the grass and sat for a long time, my chin on my knees, looking at the beech, almost willing myself to see through it. I would have loved to hear what Brother Bernard had to say as I disappeared before his eyes. And how would Giles and Hildegarde explain that away? Or maybe they wouldn't need to. Maybe Brother Bernard, too, was in on the secret.

I should have liked to linger there a little longer. It was all so different, yet somehow all so...so the same. The people spoke differently and had different customs, but at heart, I was realising, people are always the same even if centuries divide them.

Despite my stare, or maybe because of it, the tree remained solid. No vibrations. Cautiously, I stood up and touched my palm lightly to the trunk. I felt nothing unusual. It was firm and gnarly beneath my hand. I knelt down and groped for the hollow in the roots, pushing my fingers in. I could still see them. The tree was perfectly normal, like any other tree. Thank goodness I wouldn't have to shepherd a rampaging twelfth century knight, complete with sword, through the foibles of the 21st century. I wasn't sure that would have ended well.

Slowly, thoughtfully, I got to my feet, brushing the grass from my jeans. As I wandered back to the car, I saw a coach-load of tourists pull up. Glancing at my watch, I realised it was still only 10 am. I could easily spare another hour.

Making my mind up, I walked quickly to the entrance, paid over the fee and wandered in. It seemed so strange to see that beautiful old building in ruins. Strange and sad.

I hadn't had time to get much of an impression of the Abbey; I'd spent most of my time in Hildegarde's chamber and in that awful cell, but I had felt the essence, the flavour if you like, and it lingered softly like a ghost. The turnstile must be where the gates had been. I smothered a chuckle as

I remembered the vision of the porteress, Giles' hand clapped over her mouth, her eyes bulging with fury. Would she ever forgive him for that?

Trying to get my bearings, I wandered through the ruins, stopping from time to time to put my hands on the worn stone, imagining Etheldreda, with her merry blue eyes, Ursel, Hildegarde, Brother Bernard and that terrified young nun who thought I was a demon. It was hard to believe that, only a short while ago, they had been going about their business in the Abbey while I was with Giles by the beech. Now, they were nothing more than bleached bones – no grave, no headstone, not even remembered in books or hearts, except mine. It was difficult to come to terms with.

I followed the line of the interior foundations. Here would have been the cloisters and the infirmary. And here, this, I thought, was where Hildegarde's chamber had been. Standing there, nothing but a few stones around me, I tried to remember it as it had been – the ornate desk, the garderobe with its wall hanging, the punishment cell Hildegarde never used. I could almost see it still peopled by their shades. I suppose it sounds silly now, but I still felt a connection with them all.

A clamour of voices jolted me from my thoughts. The tour guide was leading the coach party to where I stood, one hand still on the wall. The group swallowed me up, and as the guide began his monotonous drone, I listened with more interest than I would have done before.

I tagged on behind, and as I followed them round, I heard the guide saying in dismissive tones, "Of course, with places like this, there are always legends which have absolutely no bearing on the truth. The villagers here insist that in the days of Richard the Lionheart, his brother, Prince John, was brought to the Abbey suffering from a mysterious malady. Apparently, a strange young woman appeared from a tree, dressed all in green like a wood nymph, and performed some kind of magical rite which instantly healed the future king.

"They say there was a hue and cry, and his men later searched the village trying to find her, terrified that word would get out and the balance of power would fall into the hands of those who wanted the boy, Arthur, to be Richard's heir. A nice story, but all rubbish of course," he said, patronisingly. "No truth in it at all. History never records John as going anywhere near the place. Popular reasoning is that the myth grew up to explain a large and rather beautiful book which Eleanor, the Queen Mother, was said to have donated to the Abbey library. Of course, there was a fire in the library some seventy years later which destroyed many of their their books, so we have no evidence that there was such a thing. But history always creates its legends."

I smiled to myself. There may be no evidence of a wood nymph, but legends have their own way of staying alive.

Turning on my heel, I walked away from the pompous guide and his flock of tourists, all listening like sheep. I had things to do.

Sitting with my mother a couple of hours later, I reached for my coffee. She started and grabbed my hand, staring hard at the ring Hildegarde had given me, her face white.

"Where did you get that ring?" I could hear a choke in her voice. Her eyes, wide and startled, bored into mine. How could I explain? I thought I'd better take refuge in a small lie.

"I saw it in a second-hand shop and just took a fancy to it."

"A second-hand shop? No way! Marion, take it off. Let me see it properly."

I slid it off my index finger and passed it to her. She took it almost reverently, turning it this way and that, peering at the inside of the ring, while I sat there gaping at her.

"Marion, this is an old family ring. I'm so sure, I'd put money on it."

I felt a tingle run down my spine.

"It belonged to my cousin, Doreen." Her face sombre, she continued, "We knew each other well, spent a lot of time together when we were young. As we got older, we couldn't meet up so often. She was pretty busy, and I had you and your brother by then. You were only a toddler, and I didn't have a car." Her lips trembled, and she wiped a tear from her eye. "She was a bit younger than me and studying medicine. It was tragic, what happened to her. She went to a party one summer. I'll never forget the date – it was Midsummer's Eve, 1975. She never arrived, and no one knows what happened to her. Her car was discovered at Sparnstow Abbey a week later, but there was no sign of her, and she was never seen again. They had search parties out and everything. It was in all the papers at the time, and I remember being really upset. She wasn't just my cousin; she was my friend."

I stared at her, mute. Then, Doreen was related to me? I look a bit like Mum did at my age. Had she recognised me? Was that why she had given me the ring? "A cousin? You never talked about her before. What happened to her parents?"

"They'd both died a couple of years before. Doreen Suttener, she was called. My uncle always said the ring was centuries old, passed down the generations. Doreen wore it all the time. She loved that ring. She reckoned she'd traced her genealogy right back, but to be honest, I don't think you can go that far back. I don't think the records were kept that long ago. I don't know. I was never much of one for history and stuff, but that's what Doreen reckoned anyway. There's no one left on her side of the family now. Doreen was the last one."

Suttener? Suttener? A flashback shot into my mind. The ring Hildegarde had slid into my hand...the ring glinting on the little finger of Giles de Soutenay's left hand as it gripped mine – they were the same. No. Surely not! Suttener? De Soutenay? I know a lot of names changed over the centuries. Was it too huge a stretch of the imagination? Why hadn't she handed it over to the Abbey when she had taken her vows? Maybe she'd always hoped to find a way to pass it back to the family. Maybe because she thought it shouldn't be in the same time as its original owner? Had she recognised it on Giles' hand and thought hers was safer out of that time? I would never know.

My mum dropped it gently back into my outstretched hand and gave me a shaky smile. "Fancy it finding its way back to the family after all this time. It's definitely the same ring. Look." She picked it up again and held it to the light, pointing to some marks on the inside. "See these? They were on Doreen's ring as well, I remember her showing me. She let me try it on once. It only fitted my index finger too, and we both had biggish fingers like yours. I think it was originally made for a man. Maybe for his little finger or something."

I slid it back onto my own finger silently.

EPILOGUE

Four Days Past Whit Monday 1217

Giles de Soutenay approached the tree carefully. Kneeling, he pulled aside the growth which had sprouted and now covered the small, hidden cleft at the base of the tree. He peered in and smiled; she had never let him down in all this time. Wonderingly, he touched the new devices which lay there. Then, he picked up the small caddy next to them and sniffed the contents for a moment. Putting the lid back on, he replaced it in the hollow. He wouldn't know how to use this herb. There was no point in keeping it.

John had died the previous October. Giles had held fast to young Henry's claim to the throne, and Henry's armies had prevailed over the French forces. There had been great cause for concern at first as the French had overpowered London and part of the rest of the country. Miraculously, they had overcome, and Giles' faithfulness would be rewarded.

The French were beaten; there was no doubt about that. There would be more battles, but victory was now assured. This was the earliest he could make his rendezvous. He had been in the thick of the fighting over Whitsuntide. Now, he had been given leave to keep his appointment. He was wearied beyond belief, but he was here.

He wondered how long the devices had been lying there. Mayhap she had only just left them.

The Abbess Hildegarde had died that previous autumn, just after John's death. Giles missed her sorely, for they had become firm friends. Etheldreda had become the new Abbess. She was kindly disposed to him, knowing some of their secrets, but they had not the warmth, almost kinship, between them that had developed between himself and Hildegarde. He missed her as though she were indeed family. Theirs had been a strange bond.

Smiling in reminiscence, he left the new devices which were waiting for him, placing the old, unused ones next to them. In all those years, John had never been stung by another bee. He had never needed the new devices which appeared, as if by magic, each year. There would be no need for them now. Next to the device and the caddy, he placed a small pot.

During Hildegarde's final sickness, Giles had visited frequently. That last time, despite the ravages pain and age had wrought on her face, her tired eyes had lit up as he'd entered her chamber. He'd sat for a while, not speaking, content to just be with her. She had raised herself upon one elbow and beckoned to him. As he bent to her, she had pointed to a painted pot in the wall recess behind the candle sconce. He'd retrieved it and brought it to her. Shaking her head, she had whispered, "For Marion." Opening it, she'd shown him the small scrap of parchment concealed within. He hadn't been able to understand the words she had scratched on it, but he guessed Marion would be able to decipher them. They looked to be of her time, not his.

Hildegarde had fallen back onto her pillow exhausted, as though that last brief spark of life had drained her. Etheldreda had motioned him to leave, and Hildegarde's confessor had replaced Giles at the bedside.

As he had taken his final leave of her, he'd turned and looked back. The lines had smoothed from her brow, and he had caught a brief glimpse of the young woman she had once been; strangely, that youthful countenance had seemed almost familiar to him. He had left the chamber to the low murmur of the priest granting her absolution. *Not that she needed it*, he decided. Hildegarde had been one of the most saintly women he had known. She had touched his life in a way no other had.

Now, Giles stood up, touching the tree's warm bark beneath his hand, feeling the life inside it. He stayed there for a few moments, both hands on the gnarled trunk. Not a breath of wind stirred the day, yet the leaves started to quiver. The tree started to vibrate, and a slight hum came from within. She was there. He let go of the trunk and watched as a hand came through and groped for the old devices.

He stooped and held her hand briefly for the last time, pushing all the devices back into her hand, stroking her palm with his thumb. Then, he guided her fingers to the caddy, hoping she would understand the significance of his actions.

"Giles?" A woman's voice called musically from the glade where he had left his horse. His wife, Isabella. Not just fair of face and temperament but possessed of a good dowry and fertile; she'd borne him four sons and two daughters living.

Giles pressed the hand beneath his once more and felt the fingers respond. He lingered a few more moments then letting go, he rose to his feet, took one last glance at the old tree and, leaving the future behind him, walked away from Marion, back to his wife, who stood waiting for him in his own time.

Out of Time

If you have enjoyed Out of Time, please consider writing a review on Amazon. It really does make a difference. Thank you.

AUTHOR'S NOTE

I had a lot of fun doing the research for this story, but I confess, I am no historian, and I was left nearly tearing my hair out over various things, as some of the information I wanted to know was quite difficult to find.

I have endeavoured to be as historically correct as possible, but this is pure fiction, so you may have to forgive me for taking a few liberties.

Try as I might, I was unable to discover whether Eleanor was actually in England at the time of my story – she was certainly in Messina in the March, bringing with her Berengaria, Richard's betrothed, but she did not stay for the wedding, which was held in May, so it is possible that she might have been where I needed her for those few days. It would certainly have been easier for me if this intrepid woman had lived sedately in England, doing embroidery, but then she would not have been the fascinating woman that she was, and she would have been a less interesting addition to my story. It has been impossible for me to find a definite date of birth for her, but it would seem that she was born between 1122 and 1124, so for the sake of my story, I have used the later date.

According to my research, John was at loggerheads with William Longchamp around about this time, but I have allowed him a few days off for the sake of my story.

With reference to Giles' pasty, pastry in medieval times was not always like the pastry we know today. Certain pastry was extremely hard and used purely as a container for the contents, but in my research I also found mention of softer types of pastry, so because I enjoy the humble pasty and couldn't bear to make Giles throw any of it away, I have made his pasty entirely edible.

The Battle of Lincoln, which took place over Whitsuntide 1217 was a real problem for me, as it would have been very difficult for Giles to have kept his appointment. Fortunately, the corresponding date in the future will be on May 24th, a few days later than in 1217, so I have allowed him to arrive at round about the same time as Marion.

Lastly, and I say this with my tongue firmly in my cheek, providing John with epinephrine does seem to have done the trick, as nowhere in history does it mention his allergy to bee stings. Maybe we will keep that piece of information between ourselves.

I have tried not to make any historical blunders, but it is inevitable that I will have got something wrong. I hope, however, that any blips I have made have not prevented you from enjoying my story.

I should like to thank my historical beta readers, Marie Cockburn and Angie Copping for their invaluable help. Any blunders I have managed to steer round have probably been as a result of their input. Any medieval morasses I managed to land in were entirely due to my own lack of knowledge.

Thanks also for the unstinting help of my other two beta readers, Heidi and Marie, both busy authors who are kind enough to guide my fledgling efforts.

Out of Time

Other books by Loretta Livingstone include

Fiction

Where Angels Tread
Beautiful and Other Short Stories
Four Christmases

Poetry

Rhythms of Life
Jumping in the Puddles of Life
Hopes, Dreams and Medals

ABOUT THE AUTHOR

Photograph of author by Nicola Louisa Sharp

Loretta Livingstone lives with her husband in a beautiful area of the Chilterns. She started writing verse originally but has now branched into the world of fiction. Her strong Christian faith often comes through in her writing. You can find more about Loretta and her books on her website www.treasurechestbooks.co.uk or at Amazon.

Loretta says of her books, "Above all, I want to leave my readers with smiles on their faces."

Printed in Great Britain
by Amazon